New Year, New Murder
A Freshly Baked Cozy Mystery
By
Kathleen Suzette

Copyright © 2022 by Kathleen Suzette. All rights reserved. This book is a work of fiction. All names, characters, places and incidents are either products of the author's imagination, or used fictitiously. Any resemblance to actual events, locales or persons, living or dead, is entirely coincidental. All rights reserved. No part of this book may be reproduced or transmitted in any form or by any means, electronically or mechanical, without permission in writing from the author or publisher.

Chapter One

"I CAN'T BELIEVE WE'RE doing this," Lucy gasped, her breath showing in a cloud of white in front of herself.

I nodded and pushed down the scarf that I had wrapped around the lower half of my face. "I know. It feels awful right now, but if we keep at it, it won't be so bad after a month or so."

She shot me a look. "A month or so?"

I nodded and huffed air out of my mouth as we ran. Maybe 'ran' was more of a euphemism for what we were doing, because it was more like trotting. "We took it easy in November and December, and now we're paying for it. With a little luck, after we run consistently for a month or so, we should be back in shape."

She groaned as we plodded along. The snowplows had come through, and the streets were clear, but the cold was biting. As I forced my muscles to move, I was rethinking running outside. A gym membership might have been a better plan. The only upside to running in this frigid temperature was that the sky was a clear, impossibly blue color, and the sun was shining. You didn't see beautiful mornings like this in a large city.

After a moment of silence, she sighed. "I don't know if I can make it a month."

"Lucy, you can make it a month. I know you can. I'm putting all my faith in you." I pulled the scarf back up over my mouth and nose. I was pretty sure my nose was about to fall off.

She groaned again. "At least you've got some faith. Because I don't. I really just want to be back in my nice, warm bed right now."

"So do I," I said, pulling my scarf down again. "But just think, come summer we're going to be in the best shape of our lives." Lucy was my best friend and hadn't been running as long as I had. But even though I had more experience, I was still having trouble motivating myself to keep going in this cold.

Lucy had taken up running with me last year, but we had gotten lazy during the holidays. We were now paying for that laziness—me with an extra seven pounds and Lucy with an extra nine—running it off was our only solution. I'm not saying it wasn't worth it, but I always hated the post-holiday weight gain and the work it took to get rid of it.

"I like these new shoes you got me for Christmas," she said, glancing down at her feet.

"I'm glad you do. I thought they were pretty cute." I had gotten her some pink and purple running shoes for Christmas, and I knew that she would love them. Not that they were my first choice, but they were darling anyway.

We huffed and puffed, and a car suddenly careened around the corner, slipping on the ice as the middle-aged driver frantically tried to stop its sliding. There was a moment that we made eye contact—his eyes were open wide as he gripped the steering wheel and mine open just as wide as I hurried to get out of the way.

"Watch out!" I called, shoving Lucy toward the side of the road.

We watched as the car regained its traction on the street and headed off without so much as a glance in our direction.

"Did you see that? He didn't even wave an apology to us," Lucy said, sounding exasperated.

"I saw that. Maybe he didn't see us out here." I knew he had, but he looked like he had been busy at the moment. Acknowledgments were for social engagements.

She shook her head. "I tell you, some people shouldn't be out on the roads."

We slowed to a walk as we headed up a hill. Neither of us was in any condition to run up it, especially in the cold. We both panted as we walked, and I was glad no one was nearby to witness it.

She turned and looked at me. "I do enjoy running, don't think that I don't. But maybe we should mix up our route? I like the running path because it's usually easy and flat, but I can't run this hill yet."

I nodded. "Don't worry about it. I'm not in any condition to run it either. But the running path is covered in snow, and we need a challenge." A blue jay flew past us and into the nearby woods.

"Says you," she said, looking at me, one eyebrow arched.

I chuckled, glancing at her. Short blond hair poked out from beneath a black knit cap, and a hot pink scarf was wrapped around her neck. "You know what we need?"

She shook her head. "I'm afraid to ask."

"We need a real challenge. Something to train for. We need to run a marathon."

Her head whipped around to look at me. "Have you lost your mind? I'm not running any marathon. I'm not in any condition to run a marathon."

"Well, I don't mean right away. We'll need some time to train."

She sniffed. "If I remember right, when you ran that marathon with Alec, all you did was complain for weeks afterward. Why do you want to run another marathon?"

She wasn't wrong. That marathon took a lot out of me, and it had thrown me off of my regular running for months afterward. "Okay, you're right. A marathon is an enormous undertaking, and I probably don't really want to do that, anyway. What about a half marathon? What do you think about that?"

"Thirteen miles?" she asked as we crested the hill. "That's a long way."

I nodded. "Sure it is, but we need a challenge, right? We don't have to do it anytime soon. Maybe next summer?" I was suddenly getting excited about the idea of a half marathon. It wouldn't be anywhere near as hard as a full marathon, and with some training, I was sure that we could be ready for it come summer.

Her breath came out in a huff, and it hung in the air as we walked. "I'm not sure I can commit to that. That's crazy talk."

I shook my head. "It's not crazy talk. We'll get on a regular program of running, and we'll do a half marathon. Alec will run with us. You know how much he loves his running." My husband was a born runner. Me? Not so much, but I had learned to enjoy it.

She smiled. "All right. Let's do a half marathon. I think."

Lucy might not have felt ready for a half marathon, but I knew she could do it. We would both put in the training from now until sometime in the summer, and we would do it.

"You won't be sorry," I said as we went back to a slow jog at the top of the hill.

Lucy opened her mouth, but before she could say anything, her foot slipped out from beneath her, and she just barely managed to catch herself before hitting the pavement. She looked at me. "Are you sure about that? Because I feel like I'm going to regret it."

I chuckled. "Come on, let's do this. We're going to run a half marathon in the summer, and we're going to have the time of our lives. Just think about how great we'll look in a bathing suit come summer."

She looked at me, one eyebrow raised. "Well, you do have a point there. If we put in all that training for a half marathon, we'll look great at the beach. I wish I could get Ed to run with us."

I chuckled. "Now you're asking for a miracle. That isn't going to happen."

She nodded. "I know. But a girl can wish, can't she?"

I nodded. "You bet."

We headed down the street and I was again thinking about a gym membership. Running in the snow wasn't my favorite thing to do, and we might be able to get more conditioning done if we got a membership at the local gym. As we trotted along, a car came up behind us, and as soon as it drove alongside us, there was a honk, and we both turned to look. It was Ed, Lucy's husband. He held up a coffee cup from the Cup and Bean, saluted us with it, and then hit the gas.

Lucy slowed to a walk. "Can you believe that? That husband of mine has some nerve."

I chuckled, breathing out heavily. "He certainly does. The least he could have done was pick up coffee for us. We could use the caffeine to help us keep running."

She turned and looked at me. "Now you really are asking for a miracle. That man isn't going to think about us. There are days that I wonder why I stay married to him."

I looked at her, one eyebrow raised. "You're not serious, are you?" Lucy and Ed complained about one another often, but I never took it seriously. That was just the way their relationship worked.

She smiled and shook her head. "No. Ed may be a pain in my behind at times, but he's a good guy. I've never felt like I couldn't trust him or like I didn't know what he was going to do next."

"It's nice to have somebody reliable," I said, thinking about Alec. I knew what I was going to get with Alec, too. He was a steadfast person, and he made me feel safe.

She nodded. "Yeah, he may be difficult at times, but I'm glad I have him."

We ran down the road and I checked my watch to see if we were close to being finished. Unfortunately, we had just begun.

Chapter Two

WE STOOD IN LINE AT the Cup and Bean and when we made our way to the front counter; I looked up at the menu board. I was a little sad that the holiday offerings were gone. We were in that coffee-lull known as January. It was the beginning of the second week, so the Valentine-themed coffees weren't available yet, and I frowned as I read over the menu board. "Well, I guess I'm just going to get a plain Jane mocha."

"You don't sound excited about that," Lucy said as her eyes went to the menu board.

I shook my head. "I miss pumpkin spice lattes and peppermint mochas. And eggnog lattes."

She sighed. "Don't forget gingerbread lattes. I guess I'll take a plain Jane mocha, too."

"Coming right up," the barista said and got to work on our drinks. I glanced over at the corner table, and Mr. Winters held up his cup of coffee in a salute. Mr. Winters, elderly though he was, knew just about everything that went on in Sandy Harbor. He was a good friend to have when investigating a murder. I smiled and nodded to him. When our coffees were done, I paid for them, and we headed over to his table.

"So, how are things going, Mr. Winters?" I asked brightly as I sat down. Lucy sat beside me and took a sip of her coffee.

Mr. Winters' eyebrows shot up. "Things? What things?"

I shrugged. "Seems like something is always going on around here. How have you been? How was your Christmas?"

He nodded. "My Christmas was satisfactory. How were your Christmases?" he asked, looking at Lucy and including her in the question.

"We had a wonderful Christmas," Lucy said, setting her cup down. "But then, my husband and I were invited over to Allie's for Christmas dinner, so you know everything was wonderful."

I smiled. "Lucy, you are the best friend I have ever had. You always love everything I make."

"Of course I do. Because it's always wonderful." She chuckled.

Mr. Winters frowned. "That's funny. I guess my dinner invitation must have gotten lost in the mail?" he asked pointedly.

Uh oh. It wouldn't pay to make Mr. Winters angry. He might not tell me what I needed to know when investigating a murder. "Oh, Mr. Winters, I didn't know you would want to come. I apologize. You'll definitely get an invitation next year."

He nodded. "Good. I will expect one. As I said, my Christmas was satisfactory. Had several of the relatives over and ate too much."

"Then you did Christmas right," I said and took a sip of my coffee. It may not have been a peppermint mocha, but it was still a mocha, and it was tasty. I took another sip.

"So, what are you two doing this morning?" he asked, eyeing us in our running gear.

"We just went for a morning run. You really should join us, Mr. Winters." I eyed him back.

He chuckled. "Now you've lost your mind. No way am I getting out in the cold and going running. Unless someone is chasing me. I'll run then."

"Oh, Mr. Winters, you're already coming out into the cold to come down here to the Cup and Bean. If you start running, it'll warm you right up." Lucy nodded.

"That's all right. I've got a heater in my car, and I get warm enough. Has anybody told you that you're out of your mind for running in the winter?"

I nodded. "Yes, I've been told several times, but that never stops me. Lucy and I are going to run a half marathon next summer, and we're in training."

He made a low whistling sound. "I guess it's official, then. You both are out of your minds."

We laughed. "That we are," Lucy said.

"I'm glad you had a good Christmas, Mr. Winters." I didn't know much about Mr. Winters' personal life. Inviting him to Christmas might have been a good idea. We might have found out more about him, especially who his sources were. Most of the time, he wouldn't name them.

"I love Christmas so much, I still haven't taken my tree down," Lucy said.

I turned and looked at her. "Are you kidding me? Your Christmas tree is still up?"

"It's January. What are you waiting for?" Mr. Winters asked, squinting. "What's the matter with you?"

She shrugged. "I guess I'm just running a little behind on things this year."

Even I was surprised that Lucy still had her tree up. "I'll say. When I drop you off, I can help you take it down. How does that sound?"

She smiled. "It sounds great. I'd appreciate the help."

We stayed and talked to Mr. Winters for a while, then headed to Lucy's house.

LUCY'S HOUSE WAS NICE and warm when we walked in. "I don't see Ed around."

She shook her head. "He had some errands to run this morning. I'm sure the Cup and Bean was his first stop, so he'll probably be gone a while," Lucy said as we headed to her Christmas tree. Just as she had said, she hadn't taken anything off it yet.

"It's always so sad taking down the Christmas tree," I said wistfully.

She nodded. "You can say that again. I'll get the totes from the closet, and we'll have this done in a jiffy." She disappeared into the other room and reappeared a minute later with two large red totes. Her tree wasn't big, so it wouldn't take us long.

"Perfect." I took a tote from her, and we began taking the ornaments off the tree.

"Look at this," Lucy said, holding up a bell made out of Styrofoam. "I made this in kindergarten."

"Are you serious?" I asked. The bell was pale blue and covered in glitter that no longer sparkled.

She nodded. "It's made out of egg cartons. I was so proud when I brought it home to my mother."

I chuckled. "I've got a few things that the kids made when they were in school, too. I treasure those items."

"Well, they're lucky. My mother said to take it with me when I moved out."

I chuckled. Lucy's mother reminded me of Ed in some ways. So I guess in some ways, Lucy married her mother.

"I love these tiny glass icicles," I said as I carefully removed them from the tree and put them back into their box.

"I love them, too. They're some of my favorite ornaments."

It only took us about twenty minutes to get the tree undecorated and the ornaments packed up. We carefully took the tree apart and put it back in its box.

"There, now that job is out of the way, and it won't be nagging at you," I said, placing my hands on my hips.

She nodded. "I can't tell you how much I appreciate that. I don't know why I was putting it off."

"Where do these belong?" I asked, nodding at the totes.

"Let's take them out to the shed." We each picked up a tote and headed to the backyard. It had snowed two days earlier, and the yard was a smooth landscape of white. We made footprints in the snow as we headed to the metal storage shed and set the totes down in front of the closed door.

She looked at the door, her eyebrows furrowed. "That's strange."

"What's strange?" I asked.

"We never lock the shed door, and somebody has locked the padlock on it."

"Maybe Ed accidentally did it the last time he was in there," I suggested.

She nodded. "Maybe. Let me run and get the key. I'll be right back."

She headed back into the house, and two minutes later she reappeared carrying the cardboard box with the tree in it. She set it next to her tote and then produced a key from her coat pocket. "Here we go. We'll get this taken care of." She put the key in the lock and twisted it back and forth. "I hope it isn't frozen." I watched as she worked the key back and forth and after a minute or so, she finally got the lock to pop open. "There we go."

She removed the padlock and pushed the sliding metal door open, and then she gasped.

"What is it?" I asked, taking a step closer and looking over her shoulder. "Oh no."

Lucy looked over her shoulder at me. "Oh no, is right."

Laying in the middle of her shed floor was a man. But not just any man, a dead man. There was a knife sticking out of his chest.

His skin was white, whether from death or from being frozen out here in the cold, I couldn't tell. I squinted. I couldn't place who it was. "Who is that?" I whispered.

She was quiet for a moment. "Well, he *was* my husband."

My head whipped around so fast I almost gave myself whiplash. "Your husband?"

Chapter Three

I STARED AT LUCY, MY mouth open. The man lying on the floor of the shed was not Ed. "What do you mean, he *was* your husband?"

She shrugged and then looked at the man. "It's Bruce Wentland. We were married once. A long time ago." She turned to me, her face expressionless.

I shook my head slowly. "What are you talking about, Lucy? Bruce Wentland? I don't even know who this guy is. When were you married to him? Are you serious?"

She nodded. "Yeah. Before I married Ed, I was married to Bruce."

I stared at her, stunned. "How do I not know this? You're my best friend and I don't know that you were married to somebody else before Ed. How come you never said anything?"

She shrugged. "It was a bad chapter in my life, and once I closed the page on that one, it was over. I didn't see any reason to talk about him."

My mind was spinning, trying to make sense of things. "How old were you when you got married?"

"Eighteen. I was just out of high school. We were both just out of high school when we got married. It only lasted six months. There's nothing to talk about." She shrugged as if it were no big deal, but it was a big deal. The dead body in her shed made it a big deal.

I shook my head again. "I don't know, Lucy. I'm kind of shocked that you never mentioned him."

"I know."

She stepped inside the shed, looking down at him. She seemed incredibly calm about it. If I had found a dead man in my storage shed, I would be freaking out. Especially if he was somebody I had been married to once. I stepped into the shed with her.

"Are you sure he's dead?" It was a dumb question, but this was shocking, and I didn't know what else to say.

She nodded. "His lips are awfully blue. Blue never looked good on him."

My eyes went to her, and I pulled my cell phone from my pocket. I quickly dialed my husband, Alec.

"Hello, beautiful," he said when he answered the phone.

"Alec, Lucy and I just discovered a dead body in her shed. It's her husband."

"Ed? Ed is dead? What happened?" Alec said, sounding rattled. I could hear the chair he was sitting on in his office squeaking as he sat up.

I shook my head and then realized he couldn't see me. "No, apparently her former husband's name is Bruce. And he is as dead as they come."

Alec was quiet for a moment. "Wait. Our Lucy? Her husband's name was Bruce? And he's dead? What happened to Ed?"

"Yes. Our Lucy. And her former husband is dead, and his name was Bruce. Ed is running errands. I guess we should have called the police and not you, but let's just say I was a little shocked when she said this guy had been her husband once."

There was silence again, and then he said, "well I guess I'm a little shocked, too. But I'm glad Ed is okay. I'll give Yancey a call, and I'll be right there." Alec was a private detective, and I felt like we were going to need him to straighten things out. I certainly didn't know what to do about this.

"That's a good idea." I ended the call and tucked my phone into the pocket of my coat. I glanced at Lucy. Her eyes were still on Bruce.

"Is he coming down?" she asked without looking at me.

"Yes. He's going to call the police, and then he'll come over here."

She turned and looked at me. "When my divorce from Bruce was finalized, my greatest wish was that I would never lay eyes on him again. But here he is."

I nodded. "Here he is. And somebody has jammed a knife into his chest. So, you haven't seen him since you got divorced?"

She shook her head, glancing at Bruce. "Not up close. But last summer, when we were at the beach, I saw him from a distance. I thought maybe my eyes were playing tricks on me, and then he disappeared into the crowd, so I figured maybe it was just a man that resembled him. I guess I was wrong. I wonder how long he's been back in Sandy Harbor?"

"I see."

She looked at me. "Don't look at me that way. It wasn't like I was going to chase him down to make sure it was him. I was just hoping it wasn't, and that he wasn't in town anymore. He moved to California after we got divorced."

"I guess that was good since you didn't want to see him again." I didn't know what else to say. I was still dealing with finding out that my best friend had been married to someone before her current husband and never mentioned it. It wasn't like Lucy was under any obligation to tell me every detail of her life, but we talked about everything. Absolutely everything. And now I was finding out there was a part of her life that I knew nothing about?

She sighed. "I would've preferred he had stayed there in California."

I didn't blame her. At the very least, he could have just stayed on the other side of town and not bothered her. But the big question was, who would kill him and leave him in her storage shed? And why?

I WRAPPED MY ARMS AROUND myself as the police officers walked in and out of the storage shed. The totes with the Christmas ornaments and the box with the tree had been pushed aside. I turned to Alec. "This is crazy."

He nodded and put his arm around me. "You can say that again. So he's Lucy's former husband?"

"That's what she says. He looks like he's been in there a while."

"That he does."

I turned back to the shed. The officers were looking around the outside of the shed now. "Where's Lucy?"

He jerked his head to the corner of the yard where she was talking to Yancey Tucker. Yancey was taking over for the chief of police while he took some time off.

Lucy looked calm, but I didn't know how she could be. I turned back to Alec. "I can't imagine who would do this. Not the murder, but the fact that they stashed his body in Lucy's shed."

Alec gave me a sympathetic smile. "It is odd. You didn't see any footprints out here in the yard?"

I shook my head. "None. It didn't look like either Lucy or Ed had been out in the yard since the last time it snowed. I guess that means the body has been there at least that long?"

He nodded. "Looks that way." He glanced back at Yancey.

"Do you think they'll have you work on the case?"

He shrugged. "I think if they were going to have me work on it, he would have me over there asking Lucy questions."

"That's what bothers me."

He turned to me. "Let's not jump to conclusions yet. How long did Lucy say they were married?" He could read me like a book.

"Six months. Right out of high school. They were both eighteen, and then he went to California after they got divorced."

"Why did they get divorced?"

I shook my head. "I have no idea. It didn't even occur to me to ask. I was still in shock over finding a body and the fact that she was married to him."

The county coroner showed up with his assistant, and one of the officers showed him to the body. The officers had already taken pictures, and the little yellow plastic triangles with numbers had been set around inside the shed. I wondered what they saw that made them mark those spots because the shed was fairly tidy, and from where I stood, I couldn't see anything interesting. There weren't any yellow markers on the outside of the shed. I wondered how long Bruce's body had been there. If Lucy or Ed hadn't gone out to the shed for quite some time, it could have been there a while.

We all turned as Ed appeared at the back door. "Say, what's going on around here?"

Alec and I headed over to him.

"Hello, Ed," Alec said calmly. "How are you this morning?"

Ed frowned. "Well, I was doing fine until I came home and saw a bunch of cops all over my house. What's going on? Where's Lucy?"

Alec sighed. "I'm afraid our wives discovered a dead body in your storage shed."

Ed's eyes got big. "What did you go and do that for?" he asked me.

I shrugged. "All I did was help Lucy take your Christmas tree down. I swear. That's all I did."

He turned to Alec. "Are you serious about this?"

NEW YEAR, NEW MURDER 21

Alec nodded. "I'm as serious as can be. You don't think these fine police officers would drop by your house just because they had nothing else to do, do you?"

Ed shook his head. "I guess not. Who's the stiff?"

I glanced at Alec. Alec glanced back over his shoulder toward the shed and then turned back to Ed, running his tongue along his chapped bottom lip. "Lucy's first husband."

Ed's eyes got big. "Her what?"

Chapter Four

IT WAS SEVERAL HOURS before both the police and the coroner left with Lucy's former husband's body. I went to the sliding glass door and looked out at the shed. It was covered in yellow crime scene tape. I sighed and turned around to look at Lucy, Ed, and Alec. Everybody had been quiet while the police were here looking around the property. Lucy had allowed them inside the house to look things over, and happily, they didn't find much of anything. I say happily because I was afraid they might be wondering whether Lucy had killed her ex-husband. In fact, we all were. It was written on our faces and I didn't even need to look in a mirror to see mine to know that.

"So? Why didn't you ever tell us that you were married before?" I sat down on the loveseat next to Alec.

Lucy picked up her cup of tea and took a sip before answering. "As I said before, it was a long time ago, and I put it in my past. Why would I bring it out again? I've never understood people who always want to talk about their past." She glanced at Ed, then turned back to her cup of tea.

Ed nodded. "It's true. She told me about it before we got married and hasn't brought it up again. I almost forgot about it."

Lucy had a point. Many people talk about their past as if it had some bearing on their present. I'm talking about things that are no longer in their lives. People who are no longer in their lives.

I nodded. "Okay. I get that. But it just seems like it would have come up in conversation at some point. I'm not trying to give you a hard time. I'm just surprised is all."

She nodded. "I know. Maybe I should have mentioned it, but it was a failed marriage. We didn't even make it a year. And I guess there's a part of me that has always felt bad about that. As if sticking out a bad marriage would've made it any better." She chuckled, but there was no humor in it.

I nodded. "I guess I can see that. Why suffer any longer than you had to? If it wasn't going to work, it wasn't going to work."

"Exactly. Look at you. You had a long, wonderful marriage to your first husband, and I predict that you will have another long, wonderful marriage with Alec. You're just that kind of person. And I guess maybe I envy you a little bit. I'm a failure at marriage." She took another sip of her tea.

"There's nothing to envy. You and Ed have been married for more than thirty years. You're not a failure at marriage." I felt bad that Lucy considered herself a failure just because she had been divorced once.

Ed looked at Lucy. "Yeah, Lucy, you're not a failure. I hung around a lot longer than that first joker did."

Lucy grinned and put a hand on his knee and squeezed it. "You sure did. You're a sucker if I ever saw one."

Ed chuckled. "You got that right."

"Lucy, do you have any idea who might have killed Bruce?" Alec asked seriously.

She shook her head. "Honestly, I was surprised when I saw him last summer. Like I told Allie, I wasn't even sure that it was him. It did surprise me to see him, but I put it out of my mind. Like I said, who wants to relive the past?"

"You don't think that Yancey thinks Lucy had anything to do with his death, do you?" I asked, turning to Alec.

Alec looked at me somberly. "He was found in her storage shed. They had a history together that wasn't good. I'm not saying that Yancey is going to jump to conclusions, but they're definitely going to take a look at her."

Lucy's eyes widened. "I wouldn't kill anybody. Alec, you need to tell him that I wouldn't kill anybody."

He nodded. "I'm sure I'll have a chance to talk to Yancey in private. I'll certainly let him know that I've known you for several years, and there's no way you could have committed the murder. But he's going to go with the evidence, and right now the evidence says there was a dead body in your shed."

"Oh no," Lucy said, looking down into her teacup. "I don't think I'd look good in an orange jumpsuit."

I looked at Alec. "So you don't think they're going to put you on the case?"

He shook his head. "Before he left, Yancey said we would talk about it. I'm not sure what he has planned."

I sighed. "Hopefully, he'll use you on the investigation. I want to know exactly what he's looking at in this case."

Alec nodded. "We all do. I took a look around while they were out there, and I didn't see a lot other than the fact that he was murdered and he was in his ex-wife's storage shed."

"Well, if Lucy had murdered him and stuck him in her shed, why would she open it up and let me see that he was there? Wouldn't she have kept me away from that shed?"

He nodded. "Of course. And it's not like I think she killed anybody. I know she didn't. I'm just telling you that this is what the police are seeing right now."

"I'll come and visit you on visiting days," Ed said to Lucy. "Allie can bake you a cake with a file in it."

She narrowed her eyes at him. "I'm not going anywhere. Don't think that you're going to be footloose and fancy-free anytime soon. I'm not going anywhere."

He nodded. "All right. I won't go new-wife shopping just yet."

She rolled her eyes and turned back to Alec. "Alec, I know you'll find Brue's killer."

He nodded. "I'll do my best. Is there anything else you can tell me about Bruce? What was he like when you knew him?"

Lucy shrugged. "He was always very sure of himself. He hated for anyone to correct him or show him up. And he drank a lot."

"Oh, I'm so sorry, Lucy," I said. "Then you shouldn't feel the least bit bad about that marriage not lasting long. That had to have been hard."

She nodded. "I know. Most people don't know that he drank as much as he did. He told them I was moody, and I was causing problems in our relationship."

I gasped. "Are you serious? He blamed it on you?"

She nodded. "He did. After we were divorced, he married Peggy Bryson. We all went to school together, and Peggy wound up pregnant by another boy from school who ditched her, so Bruce got an instant family when he married her."

"Is there anything else?" Alec asked.

She shook her head. "Not that I can think of."

"Does he still have family here in town?" I asked.

She nodded. "Yes, his mother lives here in town. Alma Wentland."

"Oh, I know her. She used to work at the bank years ago." Alma had been nice, but she was a stickler for rules. You wouldn't get far if you wanted to cash a third-party check.

She nodded. "Yes, she worked there for years. She was there when I was still in high school. She never liked me, though."

"Well, that happens sometimes with mothers-in-law," I said. "Poor thing. She's going to be getting the news that her son is dead, and that's so sad." Alma had always been pleasant toward me, so I mentally put her on my list of people to talk to.

Lucy nodded. "I never liked Alma either. She was very pushy. She liked to control her son even though we were married. She couldn't get past the fact that he wasn't her little boy anymore." She chuckled. "She would call him every morning and make sure that I had packed him a lunch for work. I told him that if he wanted, he could stop by her house, and she could make him lunch every day. He didn't like that. He didn't like being known as a mama's boy."

Ed chuckled. "Yeah, that's the thing about being a mama's boy. Word gets around, and you never hear the end of it. Not that I know anything about that." Lucy eyed him.

"So, is he still married to Peggy?" I asked.

She shrugged. "I have no idea. Like I said, they moved to California years ago, and I lost touch with him. It's not like I was about to stop by Alma's house to ask her how he was doing. I was happier with him out of my life."

I nodded. "Of course you were. Don't you worry. Alec is going to figure out what happened to him and clear your name."

Alec looked at me, one eyebrow raised. "I'm going to do all I can. Don't worry, Lucy, the police will know that you didn't kill him. Other than finding him in your shed, there isn't going to be any evidence saying that you were the one who did it."

She nodded. "I appreciate that. And I do hope that you can find out something that will get the police to look in another direction. Any direction other than mine."

We stayed and visited with Lucy and Ed for a while longer. I felt bad for Lucy. She was shaken by everything that had happened today. All I wanted was to be able to help clear her name. We were going to start with talking to Alma.

Chapter Five

"I'M NOT SURE THIS IS a good idea," Lucy said as we pulled up in front of Alma Wentland's house. It was a cute little white cottage with yellow trim. The walk had already been shoveled, and the curtains in the living room were open. I hadn't seen Alma around town in a number of years and I hoped she remembered me.

"Why not? It's good to catch up with old acquaintances, right?" I asked, needling her.

She turned and looked at me. "Have you lost your mind? You don't know Alma Wentland like I do."

"What could be so wrong with Alma?" I asked. "She's a sweet little old lady. I've known her for years." At least, I hoped she was a sweet little old lady after she saw Lucy. If Lucy's foreboding meant anything, Alma might not be sweet at all.

"Sweet little old lady? Ha! Like I said, you don't know Alma like I do." She crossed her arms in front of herself.

I grinned. "Relax. We're bringing her a cinnamon crumble coffee cake, and who doesn't like coffee cake? Besides, she just lost her son. We need to be respectful of that even if you didn't like him."

"I did not like her son." We got out of the car, and she handed me the coffee cake when I came around to her side.

"It might look better if you're bringing it to her. A peace offering."

She shook her head. "She'll probably be afraid that I slipped something in there. If I had made it, I probably would have."

We headed up the walkway. "So there is a possibility that you killed her son then?"

"Allie, that isn't funny."

I knocked on the door. "Sorry. I'll let it go."

Alma came to the door with a dishtowel in one hand. Her eyes widened. "Yes? Can I help you?"

"Alma," Lucy said, glancing at me and then turning back to her. "We heard about Bruce. We're so sorry for your loss." Lucy smiled sympathetically.

Alma pursed her lips and looked Lucy up and down. "Oh. It's you. I just bet you're sorry about Bruce."

"Hello, Alma. I don't know if you remember me, but I'm Allie—,"

She waved my words away. "Yes, yes, you're the woman who bakes. Everyone knows who you are. That red hair of yours can't be missed," she said, interrupting me.

I forced myself to smile. "Alma, I made a coffee cake for you. I'm so sorry for your loss. Can we come in for a minute?" I spoke quickly, hoping to take her attention off Lucy.

Alma turned to me, her eyes softening, and she nodded. "Sure. Come on in."

I opened the storm door, and we followed her into the house. From the entrance, I could see that the house was painted brightly in shades of yellow on the inside. The living room was a darker shade while the kitchen was a bright, cheery shade.

"I suppose you'd like a cup of coffee with that coffee cake?" Alma asked, sounding reluctant to make the offer.

"That would be lovely," I said, glancing at Lucy. I loved when we were invited in for coffee. That would give us more time to talk. It also gave me time to assess a person and figure out whether they were truly grieving or they were glad that somebody in their life had died.

We followed her into the kitchen, and I set the coffee cake down on the kitchen table and went to the coffee pot.

"Alma, why don't you sit down, and I'll pour the coffee?" I said, opening the cupboard nearest the coffee maker. I was pleased to see a neat line of coffee cups turned upside down. I took three of them down and set them on the counter.

Alma hesitated. "I hate to have you go to work in my house."

I shook my head. "Nonsense. Let me get the coffee." I quickly got to work pouring three cups of coffee and brought them over to the table.

"There's cream in the refrigerator," Alma said, not taking her eyes off Lucy. "It's your fault, you know."

I glanced at Lucy, and her eyes went wide. "What do you mean it's my fault? I haven't seen Bruce in decades. How can it be my fault?"

She shook her head. "If you hadn't left him, he would still be here in town, and whoever killed him wouldn't have had the chance to kill him."

"But he was killed here in Sandy Harbor," Lucy protested. "What difference would it make if I was with him or not?"

She shook her head, pressing her lips together as I set the cream on the table along with dessert plates and forks. I sat down in between the two of them. "Alma, I know this has to be so hard. We both feel terrible about it. Do you have any idea what might have happened to Bruce? Who might have killed him?" I poured cream into my cup of coffee, and then I cut into the coffee cake. It smelled wonderfully of cinnamon and butter.

She shook her head. "I have no idea. I just know that somebody killed him."

I pushed a plate with a piece of coffee cake over to her. "How long had he been back in town?" Alma looked the same as I remembered. Her blond hair was done in a semi-beehive, and she wore blue eyeshadow.

She took the plate from me, looking over the coffee cake. "He moved back last April with his wife and stepson, Craig. I suppose the police ought to talk to that boy."

"Oh? Why is that?" I asked.

She picked up a fork and cut into her piece of coffee cake. "Because he's no good. That boy is no good. He should've been out of the house years ago, but he's been living off of Bruce and Peggy all this time. Refuses to get a job. But yet he demands they pay for things for him." She shook her head and took a bite of the coffee cake, then softened. "Allie, this is delicious."

I nodded. "Thank you. I appreciate hearing that. So this Craig, he's still living with them? How old is he?"

"That's right. That boy never did a darn thing in his life. He's thirty-two. Not even a boy anymore. Now I suppose he'll continue living off his mother." She took another bite of the coffee cake.

I was surprised that Alma didn't show any emotion other than anger. And most of that anger was directed at Lucy. But maybe it was her way of showing grief. Maybe it was really all about losing Bruce.

"I didn't know that Bruce was back in town," Lucy said, pouring cream into her coffee. "I mean, I thought I saw him at the beach last summer, but it was from a distance, and I couldn't tell for sure."

She nodded. "Sure. They moved back home because he and his friend had begun a business, and they were getting rather successful at it. They finally decided that if they could live where they wanted, then they may as well live in their hometown, so they moved back."

"Oh? Who is his friend?" I asked.

"Darrel Peters. They started some kind of newfangled computer business of some sort. I never could figure out what Bruce was talking about."

"That's good to hear that they were successful," I said. Lucy wasn't saying anything, and it was just as well. Alma didn't seem to want to hear from her.

Alma nodded. "I don't know anything about computers. I don't know what kind of business he was up to. But they went and bought a nice house on the other side of town. Said he paid cash for it." She looked at Lucy, seemingly taunting her with this piece of information.

I was surprised. "Cash? For a house?" Bruce's business must have been very successful. I put sugar into my coffee and stirred it.

She nodded. "He said they had been very successful in their computer business. As I said, I don't know anything about computers, so I don't know what he was doing. I was proud of him for making so much money that he could buy a house for cash money."

"I'd be proud of him too," I said, glancing at Lucy. She was cutting into her coffee cake with the edge of her fork and didn't seem to be following the conversation.

"I hope you're not going to show up at the funeral," she said, eyeing Lucy.

Lucy looked at her and shook her head. "No. I have no plans to go to his funeral. I'm sure his wife wouldn't appreciate that."

"I wouldn't appreciate it, either. You were nothing but trouble for him. If he hadn't gotten mixed up with you, his life would have been completely different."

I took a sip of my coffee as Lucy gathered herself. "Really? Because you said that he had cash to buy a new house. Seems like marrying me didn't hurt him at all."

Alma shook her head. "You were nothing but trouble from the beginning. I don't know what he ever saw on you."

This was getting us nowhere. "Alma, do you have any idea who might have wanted to harm Bruce?"

She narrowed her eyes at Lucy. "This one." She nodded at Lucy. "This one killed my boy. She was jealous that he made so much money, and she killed him."

Lucy gasped. "Alma, you know that isn't true. I would never hurt Bruce."

Alma looked mad enough to spit, and I thought it might be safer to wrap this up before she did. "Well, look at the time. I'm so sorry about your loss Alma, but I think that we need to get going." I got to my feet, and Lucy did the same.

I hesitated while watching Lucy. Lucy swallowed. "Alma, I'm sorry for your loss. I really would not wish this on anyone."

We headed to the front door with Alma following after us. "You were no good. You had no business being anywhere near my son. Not ever. You'll pay for this!"

"We'll see you later," I called over my shoulder, and we hurried out to my car. When we got inside, I turned to Lucy. "I'm sorry. I didn't know it was going to be that bad."

Lucy shook her head. "It's okay. I knew that Alma never liked me. You should've come by yourself."

I felt badly for getting Lucy into this. I should've just come with Alec. "I'm sorry."

She smiled at me. "I'm just glad she didn't know that Bruce was found dead in my storage shed. I can just imagine what she would have said about that."

I chuckled. "Thank goodness, she didn't seem to know about that. I wonder why she thought you were jealous about the money Bruce was making if you didn't even know he was in town?"

She shrugged, looking out the window. "Alma's getting up there in age. She's not thinking straight."

I nodded and pulled away from the curb as Alma went back into the house and shut the door behind her.

The next person I needed to look up was Bruce's stepson. What self-respecting thirty-two-year-old still lived at home and didn't feel the need to get a job?

Chapter Six

"I HOPE WE GET SOME warmer weather soon," Lucy said as we got out of my car.

"You and me both." I wrapped my coat tightly around myself. We'd gotten a lot of snow in the last week, and I was more than ready for spring. We hurried across the parking lot to the Cup and Bean coffee shop. Inside, it was delightfully warm and smelled of fresh brewing coffee and freshly baked muffins. My two favorite things in the entire world.

"It always smells so good in here," Lucy said as we hurried to the front counter.

We looked over the menu board, and I decided on a vanilla latte and a blueberry muffin, and she went with a mocha and a vanilla bean scone. The barista whipped up our coffees in no time, and I paid for them. Lucy nodded at Mr. Winters in his usual corner table. He had his newspaper spread out in front of him and a cup of coffee sitting on the table. I nodded back, and we headed over and took a seat at his table without asking.

Mr. Winters looked up at us, squinted, and then smiled. "Well, to what do I owe the pleasure?" His white hair was neatly combed, and his cardigan was buttoned to the top button.

I shrugged as I unbuttoned my coat. "We just thought we'd stop by and have coffee with our favorite coffee enthusiast. How have you been, Mr. Winters?"

He nodded. "Been doing fine. Not crazy about all the snow of course, but in spite of that, I'm doing fine. Why do you ask?" He looked at me pointedly.

Lucy chuckled and took a sip of her coffee. "Mr. Winters, don't be paranoid. We just wanted to have coffee with you."

He chuckled and folded over his newspaper. "Heard there was a murder."

I nodded. "Yes, it was Bruce Wentland. Did you know him?"

He nodded. "Oh sure, I knew him years ago when he was a kid. He did odd jobs for my brother. Mowed the lawn, ran errands for his wife, that sort of thing. Sure is a shame that after he moves back to town, he ends up dead. You ladies know anything about it?"

I glanced at Lucy but wasn't going to bring up the fact that she had been married to Bruce. I didn't know if Mr. Winters knew that or not. "It is a shame. I can't imagine who would want to do something like that. Do you?" If I avoided his question, I couldn't let anything spill.

He looked at me, eyebrows raised. "Well, maybe. Maybe not."

"Mr. Winters, don't play coy with us," Lucy said taking another sip of her drink. "I have a feeling that you know something."

Mr. Winters chuckled again. As early in the morning and as cold as it was, he seemed to be in an awfully good mood. It usually took a while for him to warm up to the day.

He grinned. "Oh, I'm not being coy. I just thought I'd tease you girls. I haven't heard a lot about what happened to him. I do wonder though. About his business partner, I mean."

"What about his business partner?" I asked, leaning in.

He shrugged. "Darrel Peters. I knew him when he was a kid, too. Seemed like that kid was always up to something. And even when he wasn't up to something you always felt like he was. He was a sly one and always had his hand in the cookie jar if you know what I mean."

Now we were getting somewhere. "Really? So the two of them grew up together?"

He nodded. "That they did. Then they moved away to California years ago. I guess they thought they'd make their fortune there." He chuckled and folded the newspaper over again. "But I guess that didn't happen quite the way they had planned."

"And how did they plan it?" Lucy asked.

He shrugged. "They thought they had some kind of newfangled invention, and they were going to make millions. Thought they'd buy themselves homes in Beverly Hills." He laughed. "Can you imagine it? Someone from little ol' Sandy Harbor going to California and striking it rich? Buying mansions in Beverly Hills? If you ask me, they were out of their minds."

"I don't think that's such a far-fetched idea. I mean, it doesn't matter where a person was born if they've got a great idea. But Bruce and Darrel didn't have a great idea?" I picked up my cup and took a sip.

He shook his head. "Doesn't look like it. I heard they abandoned that invention they had and when into business designing websites. They got some big commercial contracts, but they were nowhere near able to buy a mansion in Beverly Hills."

"But they did well for themselves?" Lucy asked.

He nodded. "Sure. I heard they did well enough."

"What was the invention they created? The one that didn't sell?" I asked.

He chuckled. "It was some kind of spot-reducing gadget. It was supposed to tone different parts of your body, but I guess it didn't work like they thought it would."

I glanced at Lucy. "That's a shame. I could have used something like that."

She nodded. "Me too."

Mr. Winters was quiet for a moment, then cleared his throat. "I heard Darrel wanted to buy Bruce's share of the business but Bruce refused."

"Why do you think he wanted to buy him out?" I asked.

He shrugged. "I heard Darrel changed his mind about moving back here to Sandy Harbor. He liked his life there in California and it was Bruce's idea to move back. But Darrel never wanted to live around here. He had bigger ideas, so he offered to buy Bruce's share of the business so he could move back to California."

"And Bruce didn't want to do that?" Lucy asked. She glanced at me and then took another sip of her coffee.

He shook his head. "Nope. Bruce was proud of his business, and he wasn't going to sell out."

"I see," I said, taking this in. I wasn't sure if any of this had anything to do with Bruce's death, but it was something to keep in the back of my mind for later.

Mr. Winters glanced around the coffee shop, then leaned toward us. "Want to know what I think?"

I leaned forward and nodded. "Of course I do. What do you think?"

"I think Darrel killed him because he refused to sell him his share of the business."

I didn't know if it was true, but I wanted to know what his reasoning was. "Why do you think he would do something like that? There had to be easier ways of getting what he wanted."

"Like I said, the business did reasonably well. Not buy-a-mansion-in-Beverly-Hills well, but well enough. And Bruce was proud of that business. Proud of what he'd built up, as most people would be. He wanted to stay in Sandy Harbor, but Darrel was unhappy about being here and wanted to leave. I think they argued, and Darrel killed him over it."

"But it seems like it would have helped them both if Bruce would have sold his share in the business," Lucy said. "That way they both would have gotten what they wanted. Bruce would have been able to live here in Sandy Harbor, and Darrel would have been able to move back to California. It's not like Bruce couldn't start a new business here."

Mr. Winters took this in for a moment and nodded. "Sure, I guess that's true. But I heard from Bruce's wife's cousin, Mabel

Lynne, that the two of them argued about it. Bruce had no intention of selling his half of the business."

"Murder is going to extremes, though," I pointed out. "Do you think Darrel would do something like that?"

He shrugged. "Like I said, Darrel was always into trouble as a kid. I doubt he ever grew out of that. But I guess we can't jump to conclusions, can we?"

I shook my head. "No. We can't jump to conclusions, but that doesn't mean it isn't possible it happened that way. So this Mabel Lynne, does she tell you a lot?" I took a sip of my coffee. It made me warm from the top of my head to the soles of my feet.

He shrugged and took a sip of his coffee. "We were just talking. I probably shouldn't have said her name. You know I like to keep my sources to myself."

"Your secret is safe with us," I said, glancing at Lucy. She nodded.

"We need you to get more information, Mr. Winters," Lucy said. "We need to find out who killed Bruce."

He narrowed his eyes at her. "Why is this so important to you?"

Lucy sat back, her eyes widened, and then she shrugged. "You know how it is. We enjoy solving a murder."

"Are you sure that's all it is?" he asked.

I nodded. "Absolutely. Alec is on the case, and he needs all the information he can get." If Lucy didn't want Mr. Winters to know she had been married to Bruce, then I wasn't going to tell him.

He thought about this for a moment and then nodded. "All right. I'll see what I can find out."

I smiled. "Great. I knew we could count on you."

Mr. Winters was always a great source of information, and I knew he would try to find out something. I glanced at Lucy. She didn't want it spread around town that her former husband had been murdered and dumped in her storage shed. I didn't blame her. Some people might remember they had been married once, but maybe most of those people had passed away or forgotten about it since it had been so long ago.

Chapter Seven

I WATCHED ALEC AS HE put the lid on his coffee mug. "Where are you off to this morning?"

Alec looked at me, one eyebrow raised. "Oh, nowhere. I think I'll just stop by my office and take care of a little paperwork. What are you doing today? I bet you've got a lot planned."

I narrowed my eyes at him. "Don't try to change the subject. That travel mug says you're going to do some traveling. Where are you off to? What are you doing?"

He sighed and took a sip of his coffee. "I'm going to interview Peggy Wentland. There now. Are you happy? Now you know what I'm doing today. What are you doing?"

I grinned. "I'm coming with you."

Alec shook his head. "No, you're not. A woman like you has got to have something important to do. I'm sure of it."

I chuckled and grabbed a travel coffee mug from the cupboard and filled it, leaving just enough room for cream. "Not a thing. I'm free as can be. Now then, what are you going to ask her? Do you think she did it? What's going on with the case?"

He sighed. "Allie, I don't need any help today."

I turned and looked at him. "You always need my help. You know that if it weren't for me, you would never solve a case."

Alec looked at me blankly, and then he roared with laughter. "That's what I love about you, Allie. You've got such a creative mind. I've got to get going."

I grinned and hurried over to the refrigerator. "Hold on a minute." I filled the rest of my cup up with cream and popped on the lid. "Now we're ready. Let's go."

He groaned, but I followed him out the door, anyway.

THE WENTLANDS LIVED in a modest stucco home in a family neighborhood. The sidewalk hadn't been shoveled for what looked like several days, and I wondered if that was Bruce's job. We got out of the car and carefully made our way along the sidewalk to the front door. Alec rang the doorbell, and after a moment, Peggy Wentland opened the front door.

She looked at us questioningly, her eyes red and puffy. "Yes? May I help you?"

"Peggy Wentland?" Alec asked.

She nodded hesitantly. "Yes."

"I'm Alec Blanchard, and this is my assistant and wife, Allie," he said, glancing at me. "I left you a message that I would stop by today. Is now a good time to talk?"

She hesitated again and then nodded and pushed open the storm door, and we followed her inside. She motioned to the couch, and she sat on the loveseat across from us. "I just can't imagine who would want to kill my husband." Her face was haggard, with dark circles beneath her eyes and her short black hair was uncombed. My heart went out to her.

"I'm so sorry for your loss, Mrs. Wentland," I said. Peggy was short and plump around the middle. She appeared older than Lucy, and I wondered if she was, or if she simply hadn't aged well.

"Yes, we're sorry about your loss," Alec said, pulling a notebook from his coat pocket. "We had a few questions for you. When was the last time that you saw your husband?"

"On Saturday. He went fishing and left in the afternoon."

Alec looked up from his notebook. "Don't people usually go fishing early in the morning?"

She nodded. "Yes, they do. But he made a little camping trip out of it. He left in the afternoon and planned to get up early to go fishing down by Seacrest."

Alec nodded. "What about the snow? Was he camping in a tent?"

She shook her head. "No, we own a small RV. He took that. Bruce wasn't big on roughing it."

I glanced at Alec. "Where's the RV?"

She shrugged. "I have no idea. I told the officer that stopped by the other day that I hadn't seen it."

Alec nodded and made a note in his notebook and then looked up at her again. "Mrs. Wentland, did you know if there was anybody that your husband was having trouble with?"

She exhaled tiredly. "Call me Peggy. But no, I can't think of anybody that he might've been having issues with. He never mentioned anyone."

I wondered if she knew about Lucy. Had Bruce mentioned her? I didn't want to be the one to break it to her that her husband had been married previously, so I decided not to say anything. "How long have you lived here in Sandy Harbor?" I asked.

"We were both born and raised here, but we moved away years ago. We moved back about ten months ago. I was so excited to be able to move back to our hometown. Bruce was, too. California was nice, but we missed Maine. We were thinking it wouldn't be long before we would be able to retire and go to the beach every day or go camping and fishing. Bruce loved camping and fishing. I like it too, but I don't like going when it snows, so that's why I stayed home. My son usually goes with him, but he had other plans, so that's why Bruce went by himself."

"Son?" I asked. "I didn't realize Bruce had a son. I'm so sorry. I know the two of you have got to be so heartbroken." I knew about her son, but I wanted to see what she would say about him.

She hesitated, then nodded. "Yes, Craig is going to miss Bruce terribly. He's my son from my first marriage, but Bruce always considered him his own. The two were so close." Her eyes went to a framed photo of a young man on the coffee table. He resembled his mother with his dark hair and blue eyes.

"Oh, I see," I said thoughtfully. "So Craig and Bruce were close?"

She smiled. "Oh yes. They were very close to one another. Craig went camping and fishing too, but he was meeting up with some friends."

"Craig is in high school?" I asked. Alec was busy jotting down notes as she spoke.

"Oh no, he's an adult. Thirty-two. He didn't really remember Maine since we moved when he was a baby, but he wanted to move back with us." She sniffed. "I guess we should have stayed in California. Bruce would still be alive."

"I'm so sorry. This must be hard on you both. Is Craig home?"

She shook her head. "He's with friends. He's having a hard time with this, so I suggested he go do something to take his mind off of it."

Alec jotted down some more notes and then looked up at her. "So you have no idea who might want to harm Bruce?"

She hesitated. "Well, I guess there were a few issues with his business partner, Darrell Peters. Not that I think that they were huge issues, but the two of them didn't seem to see eye to eye on things anymore. Not like when they first started the business." She smiled, but it seemed sad.

"Can you think of anything in particular that happened between them?" Alec asked.

"Well, as I said, I don't think there were any serious issues, but they did have an argument or two. Bruce said that Darrell wanted him to sell his part of the business, and Bruce said he had no intention of ever doing that. Or at least not before he was ready to retire. Darrell got angry about that. He didn't want to stay here in Maine."

So what Mr. Winters had found out was true then. It made me wonder what other information he could find out about the case.

"I see," Alec said. "What kind of person is Darrell? How angry had he gotten with your husband? I'm assuming the two of you knew him well since you worked with him for so long."

She hesitated, looking away. "Well, to tell you the truth, there was something that happened a couple of weeks ago. No, maybe it was closer to a month ago," she said, thinking about it. "Darrell threatened to sue Bruce. Said he was done trying to negotiate with him. He said that the business idea was his to begin with, and it belonged to him. But that's ridiculous. Bruce came up with the idea. Darrell did have more money to put into the venture than Bruce did, but it all equaled out since it was Bruce's idea."

I was pretty sure that things didn't equal out quite like that in the business world, but I wasn't going to say as much.

"What did your husband say when Darrell said this?" Alec asked.

She hesitated, her face going pale. "He said, over my dead body. Oh my gosh. I'd forgotten all about that until you just asked. You don't suppose?" She let the question hang in the air.

"We don't want to jump to any conclusions," Alec said, sounding professional. "I will be talking with him, though. I appreciate all the information that you've given me. Is there anything else I should know?"

She shook her head. "No, that's all I can think of."

"Thank you for your time. I'll be getting back in touch with you. And again, I'm sorry for your loss," Alec said and stood up. I stood up with him, and we headed to the door. When we got in the car, I turned and looked at him. "Over my dead body? Sounds like he gave his killer a challenge."

Alec grinned. "Don't jump to conclusions. I told you that I still have a lot of people that I have to talk to."

"Oh, I'm not jumping to conclusions. I just don't like the way that sounded." Only I might have been jumping to conclusions. Who says over my dead body and then ends up dead and it turns out that the killer isn't the person that they were talking to? It made me wonder. There was a part of me that hoped that Peggy might have brought up Bruce's first marriage. Not that there was any reason she should, of course. I wondered if she even knew about Lucy. Maybe Bruce kept secrets. Lots of secrets. And maybe that was why Peggy didn't know more about who might wave wanted her husband dead. And where was that RV?

Chapter Eight

WE DROVE IN SILENCE for a while, thoughts about the case swirling around my head. "Well, what do you think?" I finally asked Alec as he drove.

He was quiet a moment, and then he shook his head slowly. "I think it's too early to know anything yet."

"I knew you were going to say that. But why would Lucy's former husband end up dead in her storage shed?"

He glanced at me, then glanced in his rearview mirror, and then turned his attention back to the road. "What are you trying to say?"

I narrowed my eyes at him. "I'm not trying to say anything. I know Lucy. She's my best friend and has been ever since we met when I moved here with Thaddeus. She's not a killer if that's what you're trying to imply."

He chuckled and shook his head. "I'm not trying to imply anything. You're the one who was asking me what I thought and brought up the fact that the dead body was found in her storage shed."

I sighed. "I know, and I'm not trying to imply that Lucy may have done something. She couldn't kill anyone." That was one thing I was certain of. Lucy may have had opinions about certain people, and she may not have liked some of them, but there was no way she was a killer. At least, I was pretty sure she wasn't.

We pulled up in front of a brick house and parked. The sky was clear now, but it was still nippy out, and I pulled my coat tightly around myself.

"You say you know her better than anyone, but you didn't know that she was married to someone else before Ed."

My head whipped around to look at him. "Okay, there's one thing that I didn't know about her. But that's all. I know Lucy. Don't try to put words in my mouth."

He chuckled lightly. "Look at you jumping to conclusions. I'm not putting words in your mouth, and I know that Lucy couldn't kill anyone. I've got great instincts, and Lucy isn't a killer. At least, I don't think so."

I gasped, but he was exiting the vehicle and missed my theatrics. I got out on my side. "Don't be funny."

"Me? Funny? I have no idea what you're talking about," he said coming around to my side of the car. We headed up the sidewalk to the front door. The door swung open before we even had a chance to knock, and standing there was a short, middle-aged man. His bald head was shining and pink from the cold.

"What's going on here?" he asked before Alec could say a word.

Alec whipped out his business card and introduced himself and then said, "we'd like to have a few questions with you."

The man hesitated, squinting at Alec, and then nodded, and we followed him inside. It was almost as cold inside the house as it was outside, and I glanced at Alec. He shrugged and shoved his hands into his coat pockets.

Alec sniffed in the cold. "Mr. Peters, I suppose you know what we're here for?"

He shook his head as he sat on the overstuffed chair across from us. "No, I don't. What's going on? Are you a cop? I don't understand. Why are you here?"

It took everything I had in me not to look at Alec. What was up with this guy? Why all the questions?

"Sort of," Alec said. "I'm working for the police department, and we need to ask you about Bruce Wentland. When was the last time you saw him?"

His eyes widened. "Why? Why would you ask a question like that? Why do you care?"

Alec was silent a moment, and I thought Darrell Peters' questions had taken him off guard as they did me. "Because that's a question we always ask when somebody is murdered."

Darrell's eyes got even wider, and he stared at Alec. "What are you talking about? Murdered? Who was murdered? Bruce?"

Alec nodded. "Yes, he was found stabbed to death a few days ago. You didn't know about it?"

He shook his head, and the look on his face said he was surprised to hear the news. I didn't know if Darrel was just a good actor or if he was truly shocked that his partner was dead. But as Bruce's business partner, how could he not know that he had been murdered?

Darrel sighed sadly. "I had no idea. No one told me. I can't imagine somebody killing him."

"Well apparently somebody had a reason to," Alec said coolly. It was clear that Alec didn't believe Darrel had no idea that Bruce had been murdered. "When was the last time that you saw him?"

He shrugged. "I guess it's been about a week and a half ago."

Alec hesitated, waiting for him to continue. When he didn't, he asked, "where did you see him, and what did you discuss?" From the sound of his voice, I knew Alec was getting irritated with him.

"He stopped by the house, and we talked about business. There's a new project that we were thinking about taking on, and we were going to make a bid on it. We hadn't worked out all the details yet, and he came by to see where I was on it."

"Did he say anything unusual? Did he say where he was going after he talked to you?" Alec pulled a notebook from his pocket and began jotting down notes.

He shook his head. "No, it was a brief meeting. Fifteen minutes, twenty tops. We just talked about the project, and then he said he was going to run some errands. Someone really killed him? It seems unbelievable."

"It's odd that you didn't know about it," I said. "Didn't you wonder where he was for the past week and a half?" I wasn't buying his act. He had to have known Bruce was dead.

He shrugged and sat back in his chair. "Not really. We both have our own projects to work on, and we usually meet up now and then to see how things are going. And that's what happened. I did think it had been a few days longer than it normally is in between talking to each other, but I just figured he had something he was working on. If he's not bugging me about something, who am I to complain?"

"So he bothered you about things?" I asked. I pulled my coat tighter around myself. How on earth was he managing to live in this house with it being so cold?

He shrugged. "We've been in business together for a lot of years. Sometimes we get on one another's nerves. You know how it is."

"No, I don't know how it is," I said. "Why is it so cold in here?"

He chuckled. "I smelled gas earlier, and the gas company is coming out tomorrow to check on the lines. I thought it would be best to shut it off for now."

I nodded, but I wasn't sure if he was telling the truth. There was something about him that told me that he might be playing a little game here. "I thought the gas company comes out immediately if there's a gas leak?"

He grinned. "I told them there was only a slight smell, and I'd shut things off myself."

He was lying. Something was wrong with him.

"So, in general, how was your relationship with your business partner?" Alec asked, looking up from his notebook.

He shrugged. "Like I said. We were in business for a long time, and sometimes we got on each other's nerves. We've known each other since we were kids. We grew up here in Sandy Harbor, and we've always been that way. We get along great until we don't, and then we just go our separate ways for a few days, and when we come back together, we're friends again."

Alec considered this and then nodded slowly. "So no one bothered to tell you that your business partner and longtime friend was dead?"

He shrugged. "Like I said, this is the first I'm hearing of it."

"That seems odd," I said, leaning forward. "It seems like someone would make sure you knew." This guy was a liar if I ever saw one.

"Yeah, well, I guess you could say that me and his wife don't get along."

"Do you know if he was having trouble with anyone?" Alec asked.

He hesitated. "Well, I hate to gossip, and maybe I shouldn't say anything at all, but I know that he and his wife were having some problems."

I leaned forward again. I needed to look into his eyes to see if he was lying.

"What kind of problems?" Alec asked.

"He told me a couple of months ago that he was ready to leave his wife. They were married for a long time, and she's got that boy that is never going to grow up and leave the house. He and the kid never did get along, and now that he's an adult, Bruce wanted him out of the house so he didn't have to deal with him, but his wife wouldn't make him leave."

"So he didn't get along with his stepson," I said thoughtfully. "Why didn't Craig want to move out? Most young men want their freedom."

He smirked. "Video games. The kid plays all day, and Bruce couldn't stand it. His mother came to his defense and said the games help him stay calm. He has anger issues. Anyone knows that violent video games aren't going to help with anger issues. So Bruce gave her an ultimatum. Either she made the kid get out of the house and be an adult, or he was going to leave her."

"That might have been very expensive for Bruce," Alec pointed out. "Since they'd been married for a long time, and he'd owned the business for the same amount of time? She probably would have left with a lot of the money. And maybe even part of the business."

He looked uncomfortable now. "Yeah, yeah. That was why he didn't jump on it immediately. He was hoping his wife would change her mind and make that kid straighten up and get out. I guess that's what he was waiting on."

Again, I felt like he wasn't telling the truth. His eyes would dart away when he answered, and there was something about him that almost seemed smug. What did he have to be smug about? That was the question.

We stayed and talked to him for a few more minutes but didn't learn anything new. When we got into the car, I turned and looked at Alec. "That house was freezing. I don't buy it that he was waiting on the gas company to fix a gas leak."

He looked at me as he started the car. "What do you think? He's got bodies in the basement? He's trying to keep them cold?"

I nodded. "Could be. You never know. But I still feel like he's lying. The gas company doesn't just tell you to shut the gas off if you've got a leak. They come out and fix it. And how could he not know that his business partner was dead? Bruce's wife would have called him and told him."

He nodded. "You're right. I think he's lying, too."

I didn't know what was going on with Darrel Peters, but I was going to get to the bottom of it.

Chapter Nine

IT WAS FOUR DAYS LATER when Lucy and I decided to stop by the grocery store after our morning run. I'd had blueberries on my mind. Reworking my blueberry streusel muffin recipe was at the top of my baking list, and I had seen that blueberries were on sale in the grocery store ad.

I pushed the buggy down the produce aisle with Lucy at my side. Everything looked shiny and fresh. There was something about produce that made me want to buy some of everything.

"Oh look, they've got oranges in," Lucy said, nodding at the large display of California navel oranges.

I shook my head. "I don't know what it is about grocery store oranges, but they're never very good. When I grew up in Alabama, my grandmama had a tree that grew the best navel oranges I've ever tasted. Each orange dripped with juice so sweet it tasted like honey."

"Don't make me jealous," Lucy said, turning to me. "I've always wanted to have an orange tree, and I even planted one a couple of years after Ed and I were married. Ed laughed, of course, you know how he is. And he was right to laugh because the thing shriveled up and died in the winter." She clucked and shook her head. "When we retire, I think we need to move to Florida or California. Then I can have all the oranges I want."

"It's not a bad idea. Then you won't have to put up with the snow," I said as I stopped in front of the display of berries. Blackberries and raspberries were also on sale, but I had my eye on the blueberries.

"My, those blueberries look good. They're so plump," she said, leaning over the plastic clamshell containers of blueberries. "I should try to grow blueberries."

I grinned. "Well, if you do, I'm coming over to raid your blueberry bushes. You hear me?"

She nodded. "I'll grow a few extra so you can make me some muffins and pies."

I picked up one of the packages of blueberries and looked them over. I didn't see any smashed or moldy ones, so I put it in my cart. Then I picked up two more of them. These weren't the little flat containers with just a few ounces of berries in them, these were the big ones that held a pound of blueberries. I was partial to blueberries, so I was pretty sure I was going to sit and eat them by the handful in front of the television tonight. Maybe I would share a few of them with Alec. Or maybe not.

Lucy looked at me, one eyebrow raised. "My, that's a lot of blueberries. What are you planning on making?"

I shrugged. "Blueberry muffins. Maybe even a blueberry pie."

"Well, don't forget your best friend," she said as we moved on to look at the apples and pears.

"I would never do that," I said, and then I spotted someone. Standing on the other side of the display looking at the pears was a familiar face. Not a familiar face that I knew, but one that I'd seen before in a photo sitting on Peggy Wentland's coffee table. I elbowed Lucy and nodded in the young man's direction.

Her brow furrowed, and then she looked at me quizzically and shrugged, shaking her head.

I mouthed to her, Craig Foster. She shook her head slowly, not understanding. I mouthed the name again, and she shook her head again. I sighed and rolled my eyes at her and did it very slowly, and then she caught on her eyes widened.

"Sure was an awful thing that happened to Bruce Wentland," I said loudly.

"Oh yes," Lucy said, watching me. "I remember him from school. Sure was a nice guy. I can't imagine anybody wanting to kill him."

I made a loud clucking sound, and Craig looked at me. "I can't imagine who would have the heart to kill someone. I don't understand murderers. It's a terrible shame." Craig seemed to go pale. "Did you know Bruce Wentland?" I asked him.

His eyes got big, and he glanced behind himself, wondering if I was speaking to someone else. But there was no one standing behind him, so he turned and looked at me again and shrugged. "Who did you say?"

"Bruce Wentland," I said, enunciating slowly. He had to know we were talking about his stepfather, didn't he? Or had I made a mistake? I came around to the other side where the pears were. "My, these pears sure do look good. You aren't from around here, are you?" I asked him.

He took a step back, looking uncomfortable about the fact that I had picked him out and was asking him questions, but

I didn't care. If he had answers about his stepfather's murder, I wanted to get to the bottom of it.

He swallowed and shook his head. "Well, I was born here, but my family moved away a long time ago. We just moved back last year." He picked out another pear and put it into the plastic bag in his hand, and tied the ends into a knot.

"Really?" Lucy asked, coming to stand beside me. "Well, welcome back. I didn't get your name."

He looked up at us as if we were out of our minds. Maybe we were, but we were going to get answers.

"Oh, my name is Craig Foster. I'm sure you don't remember me. I was a baby when I left." He moved another step away from us.

I chuckled, trying to sound friendly. "Of course not. But it's nice having an old Sandy Harbor resident move back to town. I moved a step closer, and now he was standing in between Lucy and me. He had one of those small plastic shopping baskets over one arm, and he put the bag with three pears into it.

"Well, thanks for the welcome back. I guess I had better run."

"Sure is a shame about Bruce Wentland," Lucy said again and took a step closer. "Did you know him?"

He nodded. "Well, now that you brought up his name, he's my stepfather. And it is a shame that somebody killed him. Doesn't make any sense to me." He shifted the shopping basket to his hand.

"Oh no," I said and put one hand on his arm. "I am so sorry. I had no idea that we were talking to one of his relatives. Please forgive us. We're just amazed that somebody would want to kill him." Okay, so it was a lie, but I couldn't help myself.

He shook his head, smiling uncomfortably. "No, don't apologize. My mother and I are just as shocked as anyone else is." He cleared his throat. "We've talked to the police several times, though, and I'm sure they'll find the killer soon."

I nodded. "We have the best police in the state of Maine in this town. That's one thing I do know. And they will find your father's killer." I made the mistake on purpose to see what he would say.

His brow furrowed. "Bruce wasn't my father. I mean, he was the man that raised me. So yeah, I guess he is my father. But technically, he's still my stepfather." He took another step back.

"I sure hated to hear about what happened to him," Lucy said.

He sighed, realizing that he wasn't going to get away from us or away from the subject. "It's a horrible thing that happened to him. I can't imagine who would kill him. Bruce was a great guy. Really great. We did a lot of things together. We both loved baseball, so we spent a lot of time going to games when I was younger. I was looking forward to traveling to Boston with him to catch a Red Sox game, but we never got a chance to," he said, looking away.

He was saying kind things about Bruce, but there was something about him that made me wonder. Why didn't he immediately say that he knew who Bruce was? Not only did he know who he was—he was his stepfather. "I'm so sorry about that. It's nice that you had such a great relationship with your stepfather. Sometimes stepparent and stepchild relationships aren't that good. I'm sure he will be greatly missed by you and your mother. Do you have other siblings?"

He shook his head. "No, no other siblings. It was just me and my mom and my dad. My stepdad. We've always been a tight little family."

Lucy shook her head sadly. "What a shame. I feel so bad for you and your mother. But I'm glad to hear that you had a good relationship with Bruce. I love to see happy families."

He nodded. "Oh yes, we were a happy family. We did everything together. He used to take me camping when I was a kid. Camping and fishing are another of our shared interests." He looked over his shoulder and then back at us. "Well, it was nice meeting the two of you, but I've got to run."

I nodded. "Again, I'm sorry for your loss," I called as he hurried out of the produce department. I turned and looked at Lucy. "There's a liar if I ever saw one. I told you what Darrell said about him and Bruce not getting long."

She nodded. "Yep. I bet he's not only a liar, though. I bet he's a killer, too. He may be saying nice things about Bruce, but there's something about him that makes me think he's a killer."

I had to agree with Lucy.

Chapter Ten

ALEC SUGGESTED THAT we have Lucy and Ed over for dinner that night. I was a little hesitant, only because I wondered how he was going to handle things. Alec loved Lucy and Ed as much as I did, but the fact remained that a dead body had been found in their storage shed. A dead body who was once married to Lucy and Lucy had mysteriously forgotten to tell any of us about him. Anybody except for Ed, who had forgotten about him completely, which didn't surprise me much. But still, why hadn't she at least mentioned him?

I made roast beef with potatoes and carrots for dinner, and for dessert, we were going to have a French vanilla cake with orange buttercream frosting. I loved the cold weather for only one reason. Hearty meals were appreciated and expected. This gave me an excuse to make some of my favorite dishes, and nothing beat roast beef for dinner and a decadent cake for dessert. I had scraped the inside of a vanilla bean for the cake and sprinkled thin curls of candied orange peel on top. I could hardly wait to dig in.

"This kitchen smells delicious," Alec said, walking in from the hallway. "I'm starving. I hope you made enough food."

I turned to him. "Of course I did. There's only the four of us." I removed the potholder mitts from my hands and laid them on the kitchen counter. "You're not going to grill Lucy, are you?" I knew he needed answers, but I wanted him to go easy on her.

His brow furrowed. "Grill her? Why would I grill her?"

I sighed. "You know why. Her dead ex-husband found in her storage shed? That's got to be bugging you."

"You mean, is it bugging me as much as it's bugging you?"

I nodded. That was the truth, wasn't it? "Yes. It's bugging me. Tell me it's not bugging you, and maybe I'll be able to let it go."

He shook his head. "I can't tell you that because it is bugging me. But clearly, somebody was trying to set her up. Right?"

I nodded. "Clearly. There's no other reason that body would be in her shed. I know my friend, and I know she did not kill anyone."

He hesitated, and that worried me. "I agree with you," he said.

I nodded. "Don't you think it's odd that Darrell Peters didn't know his business partner had been murdered?" I needed to change the subject. Lucy was innocent.

"I checked into that. It's true. Peggy wasn't speaking to him because she doesn't like him, so she didn't tell him."

I sighed. "That's odd. They're all a bunch of odd people."

He chuckled. "I can't argue with you." The doorbell sounded.

"Let me get that." I hurried to the front door and opened it to find Lucy and Ed standing on the doorstep. "There you two are! I'm so glad you could make it."

"Are you kidding me?" Lucy asked. "I wouldn't miss dinner at your house for the world. Home-cooked meals by one of the best cooks and bakers in town? No way would I pass on it."

"You can say that again," Ed agreed as I showed them to the hall closet to hang their coats.

"You both are too kind. I think I'm going to keep you both around a while. You're good for my ego." I may have sounded relaxed, but my stomach was turning. The longer this case dragged on, the more chance there was that Lucy might be blamed for the murder. But there were still too many questions that needed answering. There had to be a rational explanation for Lucy's dead ex being in her shed.

Lucy chuckled, and we headed into the kitchen.

"Oh, it smells so good in here," Lucy said. "What can I help you with, Allie?"

"If you'd like, you can set the table," I said as I opened the oven door to take another look at the roast. It was juicy and brown with the fat on the top of it caramelizing. "I think we're ready to eat."

Lucy went to the cupboard and got the plates and glasses out, and took them over to the table. "I hope you made a nice big roast because I don't think I'll be satisfied with just a small portion," she said as she placed the dishes on the table.

Alec chuckled. "I said the same thing." He went to the refrigerator and got the chilled bottle of wine out, and brought it to the table.

"Allie, why don't you come over to our house every day and make dinner for us?" Ed asked, leaning against the counter.

I chuckled as I put the roast onto the counter to rest. "As much as I'd enjoy doing that, I can't. I've got too many things to do around here."

He shrugged. "Suit yourself. But you know you wouldn't have anyone more appreciative of your cooking than us."

"You can say that again," Lucy said as she went to the silverware drawer to get the flatware out. She turned and looked at Alec. "Alec, what's going on with that murder case? Have you found the killer yet?"

Alec was in the middle of uncorking the wine, and he hesitated. "No, not yet. But you know how it is. For some reason, killers don't just jump out of the woodwork and confess their crimes, so I'll have to keep working on it."

She nodded. "Figures. I don't know who would want to kill Bruce Wentland, but he probably had it coming. Oh, wait. I do know who might want to kill him. Me." She laughed, and Alec and I turned and stared at her. She saw the looks on our faces and shook her head. "What are you two looking at? It's a joke. I'm joking."

"You shouldn't joke about things like that," I said. When you find a dead man in your storage shed, it was best not to kid about wanting the victim dead.

"What do you mean?" she asked, looking from me to Alec. "I was just joking, like I said."

I nodded. "Of course you were, Lucy," I said as I got a serving platter out for the roast.

Lucy looked at Alec. "Alec, you believe me, don't you? I was just joking. You know that I would never kill anyone, right?"

Alec nodded. "Of course I do, Lucy. Allie and I said exactly that earlier."

Lucy hesitated, forks in one hand, spoons and the other. "What do you mean you said that earlier? You had to discuss it? You had doubts about whether I might commit murder?"

I turned and looked over my shoulder. "Lucy, we know that you wouldn't kill anybody."

"Yeah, honey, we know that you would hire somebody to do the killing if you wanted someone dead," Ed said with a straight face.

Nobody laughed.

"Ed, shut up," Lucy said. "I think they really believe that there's at least a possibility that I could have killed someone. Right? You believe that I could kill someone?"

I turned around to face her. "Lucy, no. We know that you did not kill anybody."

"Except there's that detail about a dead body in your storage shed," Alec said in his detective's voice. I cringed when I heard it. He wanted answers, and these were answers that I didn't even want anybody to ask about. Lucy couldn't have done it. She just couldn't.

Lucy turned to him, her hands gripping the flatware. "I already told you. I have no idea how he ended up there. I haven't seen him in decades except for when I saw him at the beach six months ago. But like I said, I wasn't that close to him, and I thought that I may have made a mistake. This is ridiculous. I never killed anyone."

Alec studied her face and then nodded. "And that's what we know. We know that you did not do it."

"Except there is that weird detail about him being in our storage shed," Ed said. "I can't imagine how that happened. I guess we should keep it locked."

We all looked at him. He wasn't being as supportive of Lucy as she would've appreciated, I was sure.

She sighed. "Ed, shut up. I don't have any idea how he ended up in there. Nobody knows. Weren't there any fingerprints?" she asked Alec.

"There were a couple that didn't match yours or Ed's, but we don't have any matches on them yet," he said.

Ed nodded. "There, Lucy, you see? The fingerprints don't match ours. We're not the killers."

"What about the ones on the knife? There had to be some on the knife, right?" Lucy asked, ignoring Ed.

He shook his head. "No, there weren't any. The killer was probably wearing gloves. We'll get it sorted out."

She nodded and brought the flatware to the table, and began laying them out at each place. "I just can't imagine who would do this. Why would they leave him in my shed? It doesn't make any sense to me. Why would somebody try to set me up like that? That's what they're doing, right? His ending up in my shed couldn't be a random occurrence." She didn't look at anybody as she spoke.

"No, I don't think it could happen randomly," Alec said. "Is there anyone that you're having trouble with?"

She turned and looked at him. "Sure, his mother, his wife, and anybody related to him. Take your pick."

He nodded. "Sometimes when you get a divorce, it's best to leave all the family members behind."

She nodded. "It certainly is. Especially that family. Every one of them is a nut. But they're out of my life and have been for years, right? There's no reason why they would want to set me up by stashing Bruce's body in my shed." She headed back to the utensil drawer to get some knives.

Alec and I exchanged glances. The atmosphere had gotten stiff and uncomfortable. I brought the roast and vegetables to the table, and we sat down while Alec poured wine.

"Allie, this all smells delicious," Ed said as he helped himself to the roast beef.

Chapter Eleven

"I'M SORRY, ALLIE. I won't be able to make it to go running today. I'm feeling a little under the weather."

I looked at my phone and saw that Lucy had left the message at nearly midnight. I felt a little unsettled. We had gotten into the habit of going running together first thing in the morning and then stopping by the Cup and Bean for a coffee. After Alec had talked to Lucy at dinner, I was worried about her. The rest of the evening had been uncharacteristically quiet for us throughout the evening, and they had left early. I knew in my heart that Lucy couldn't have killed Bruce. She wasn't that kind of woman. There were just so many unanswered questions at this point. Who would kill Bruce and then stash him in his ex-wife's shed? And why?

I dozed off for a while and woke up again at 7:30. The sun was shining, but I wasn't in the mood to run, so I got up and got dressed and headed down to the Cup and Bean to see if Mr. Winters had found out anything. I also needed a shot of caffeine. In spite of having slept an extra hour and a half, I felt groggy.

The Cup and Bean was warm and cozy and smelled heavenly when I walked through the door. There was a short line at the counter, and after waiting a few minutes, I ordered a caramel latte and then headed over to the corner table where Mr. Winters sat with his newspaper and a cup of black coffee. I slid into the chair across from him and smiled as I took a sip of my coffee.

He looked up at me, his glasses perched on the end of his nose, and nodded. "Good morning, Allie. What brings you out at this hour?"

I shrugged. "It's after eight o'clock. It's not that early."

He nodded. "I guess you've got a point there. I was late getting here, but I keep forgetting that, and I feel like it's earlier than it is. Where's your sidekick?"

I sighed. Did I tell him everything? I hated to talk about Lucy when she wasn't present. It felt too much like gossip, and the last thing I wanted to do was gossip about her.

I decided to tell him as little as possible. "She wasn't feeling up to running this morning. So, what have you found out?"

He leaned forward. "Don't you think it's odd that the dead man was found in Lucy's storage shed? And that they were married once?"

I sighed and nodded. This detail was getting around now. "Yes, I think it's very strange. But obviously, someone is trying to set her up. You know as well as I do that Lucy would never do anything to hurt anyone." I said it as forcefully as I could. I had no doubts about my best friend.

He gazed at me and then nodded. "If you say so."

I gasped. "Mr. Winters! Of course, I say so. Don't say it like that."

"Like what?"

"Like you don't believe me. You do believe me, don't you?"

He nodded. "Of course. I'm sure that if you had been running around with a killer all these years, you would've known it."

"I certainly would." I sat up straight and glanced around the coffee shop. No one was sitting close enough to overhear our conversation. "Did you find out anything?"

He nodded and folded his newspaper over. "Indeed, I did. It seems that Bruce's stepson, Craig, didn't like him."

Now we were getting somewhere. "Exactly what did you hear?" I leaned forward in eagerness, waiting for his answer.

"I heard the two argued a lot, and occasionally it came to blows." He looked over the top of his glasses as he spoke. "His wife was very angry at him about it. She blamed him for the trouble they were having."

"I heard that Bruce wanted his stepson to move out. And that he was angry and upset about it." This seemed to agree with what Darrell Peters had said about him.

He took a sip of his black coffee and set the cup down. "Well, it seems that it was more than just a slight family squabble or disagreement over little things. It seems that things got rather serious between the two of them, and a neighbor called the police to break up an argument about three weeks ago."

My mouth dropped open. "Are you serious? The police were called?"

NEW YEAR, NEW MURDER 73

He nodded. "They sure were. Must've been a humdinger of an argument."

"You're telling me," I said, thinking about this. Alec could look into it to make sure the police really were called. I wondered if there were notes in the police report about what the argument was about. This was getting interesting. In fact, this was the best piece of news that I'd heard yet. If Bruce and his stepson had those kinds of issues, then maybe his stepson killed him. I couldn't wait to get home to talk to Alec.

He took another sip of his coffee and set the cup down again and gazed at me again.

"What?" The way he was looking at me said that he had something else to say.

"The thing is, if his stepson killed him, and right now my money is on the stepson, how did he end up in Lucy's storage shed? How would the stepson know anything about Lucy? And even if he knew that Bruce had been married to her years ago, how did he know where Lucy lived? Why would he bother with leaving the body in her storage shed?"

I scowled. "Mr. Winters, you just ruined things for me. A minute ago, I was sure that Craig had to have done it, and now you're poking holes in my theory."

He shook his head. "I'm not poking holes in it. We just need to make sure all the bases are covered. It's something to think about though, isn't it? Did he hate his stepfather enough to kill him? And would he go to the trouble of dragging his body over to Lucy's storage shed and tossing him inside? With the winter snow, he could have been in that shed for a while, since his wife hadn't seen him for a few days. The body wouldn't have smelled.

But why? Why drag it over to Lucy's shed? Why wouldn't he just take it out into the woods and leave it? Or even out onto the beach and leave it there for the waves to drag out to sea?"

I groaned and sat back in my chair. "You've got a point there. But that still doesn't mean that he didn't do it. If Craig was having frequent arguments with him and the police were called, then it makes sense that he's the killer. He obviously wanted to set Lucy up. If the police were looking at her, then they wouldn't be looking at him. If he could put enough doubt in the minds of the police by doing that, he could get off scot-free."

Mr. Winters thought about this for a moment, then nodded. "Fair enough. That's certainly a possibility. I haven't seen the kid myself. Is he a big guy? Could he have dragged Bruce's body into the storage shed? And were there any drag marks in the snow?"

I shook my head. "No, it snowed the night before, and Lucy and Ed rarely go out to their storage shed. They use it for things they don't use often, like Christmas decorations. If the body had been there for a few days, the fresh snow would have covered the drag marks." We needed to talk to Craig again. Just because he said he and Bruce were close didn't mean it was true.

Mr. Winters nodded and picked up his cup of coffee. "There are still a lot of questions to be answered."

"There are. Who did you get this information from?"

He raised one eyebrow. "You know that I can't give out my sources. Or at least I rarely do. But I know this information is good. It's from one of my best sources, after all."

I picked up my cup of coffee and took a big swallow, smiling as the sweet goodness rolled across my tongue and down my throat. There was something about that first cup of coffee in the morning that made me insanely happy. But I had work to do. I had to check up on Lucy and see if she and I were okay, and I had to talk to Alec to see about talking to Craig. So many things to do and so little time to do it. I got to my feet, picked up my cup of coffee, and slung my purse over my shoulder. "Mr. Winters, as usual, it's been a pleasure."

He nodded and picked up his newspaper. "As usual."

"See you later," I said and headed toward the front door. Things were starting to come together.

Chapter Twelve

JUST AS I GOT TO MY car, Alma Wentland pulled into the spot next to me. She waved at me and got out of the car. "Allie? How are you this morning?"

I nodded and pulled my coat closer around me. It may have been a sunny day, but it was still chilly. "How are you doing, Alma? I've been thinking about you."

She nodded and came to stand beside me. "I appreciate that. It's been so difficult trying to get through each day. I just can't get over the fact that my son is gone."

"It's the worst thing that any parent goes through," I said in agreement. "Do you have any other children, Alma?" I realized that I didn't know much about Alma and whether she had more children.

She nodded. "Yes, I have another son. Todd. He's flying in from Florida for the funeral tomorrow. He's just beside himself and can't understand who would want to kill his brother. Of course, I'm the same way. There's no reason for anybody to harm my son, and yet they did." She sniffed.

"I'm so sorry," I said. "I know that Alec is doing everything he can to find his killer."

She nodded. "You know, I've been thinking about things, and with all the memories that Bruce's murder has stirred up, Lucy keeps coming to mind."

My heart sank. "Lucy? What do you mean?"

"Bruce loved her with every bit of his heart. He was so broken up when that marriage fell apart. She was all that he talked about for several years after. Even when he met his current wife, Peggy, he still had Lucy on his mind."

"That's sad. He was married to another woman, but he was still thinking about Lucy?" That was no way to begin a new marriage.

She nodded. "Yes, I don't know what he saw in her myself. She talked too much, and she was money-hungry."

I didn't like where this conversation was going. "Lucy and I have been friends for a long time, and she may be abrasive at times, but she means well. She's got a heart of gold."

"Well, I certainly never saw that," she said dryly. "All I saw was the Lucy who was intent on breaking my son's heart. And that's exactly what she did. He never did get over her, not that I could see what he saw in her."

Of course, she wouldn't see it. Most mothers think that no one is good enough for their son. And now that her son was dead, I was sure the feelings were intensifying, and things may not have been as accurate as she was remembering them.

"I'm so sorry," I said for a lack of anything more helpful to say.

She crossed her arms in front of herself. "I just think it's odd that his body was found in her shed. I know that little detail now. It's funny how Alec didn't tell me that to begin with."

I gazed at her. If she was going to start making accusations against Alec, then I was going to have to get in my car and leave. I wasn't going to listen to her badmouth my husband, nor did I want to get in the middle of anything and inadvertently make things harder for Alec in some way. "Oh? I didn't realize that." I glanced at my watch. "Oh my, look at the time. I probably should get going."

"I know that Lucy is your friend. And I know that you don't want to see anything bad about her, but I believe she killed my son."

I hesitated, my hand on the car door handle. "Why? What would be her motive after all these years? She hadn't even been in contact with him after he moved back to Sandy Harbor."

She glanced away. "I'll admit that I don't know why she would do it now, after all these years. Honestly, I would've thought that she would have done it back when they were still together if she was going to do something. But that Lucy is a wily one. She's always up to no good, and I'm certain that she killed my son."

"The police can't go on hunches," I said, trying to sound as neutral as I could. "I know that you're grieving, and I know you want justice for your son. And believe me, the police want it too, and they're going to do everything they can to find his killer."

She pursed her lips. "Do you know why she left my son?"

I held back the tired sigh that threatened to escape my lips. "No, I don't know why. Why did she leave?" And then I realized that I really didn't know. Lucy hadn't said why they had split up, other than Bruce drank a lot.

"Money. That Lucy is a moneygrubbing woman, and my poor Bruce didn't have a very good job when they were married. But he had potential, and I told her that many times. In fact, look at the business that he started. They're doing quite well for themselves now, and if Lucy hadn't been so greedy, she could have been enjoying the fruits of his labor."

I nodded, turning toward my car. "Mrs. Wentland, I've got to get going now. I'm so sorry for your loss."

"I think she killed him because she wasn't over him, either."

I turned and looked at her. "What are you talking about?"

"She may say that she was over him and never had any contact with him, but I know different."

I closed my eyes for a moment, trying to gather my thoughts. "And how do you know this?" She was wrong. Lucy wouldn't lie about something like that.

"Because he told me. He said he ran into her at the grocery store, and they talked. He said that she hadn't changed since they were kids and that he wondered what she saw in Ed. That Ed is a loser. Everyone has always known that. And she told Bruce that they should get together for dinner sometime. Does that sound like she was over him?"

I could feel my cheeks get hot. There was no way that Lucy would have lied about something like this. Why would she? She said she'd seen him across the beach about six months ago, and that was the truth. I was sure of it. "Then why would Lucy tell a different story?"

She shrugged. "Maybe they did get together. Maybe that's how he ended up in her storage shed. Maybe she was going to take him out into the woods and leave his body but never got around to it."

I was starting to feel a little sick to my stomach. But if that were the truth, why would Lucy lead me to the storage shed? "You don't understand. I was with Lucy when we discovered his body in the storage shed. If she had put him out there, she wouldn't have wanted me to see him."

Her eyes widened a bit. "But you just acted like you didn't know he was found in her shed."

"Did I? Look, Mrs. Wentland, I know Lucy. She isn't a killer, and as I said, she wouldn't have wanted me to see his body if she had anything to do with his murder."

"Well, I suppose she has her own motives for letting you see his body. You'll have to ask her why she would do something like that. Maybe it was an attempt to make herself look innocent. As if she didn't know he was out there. The police would ask that same question, and she would say that if she had killed him and put him in her shed, why would she let you see him?"

My heart started to pound. This couldn't be true. No. I didn't have time for this, and I didn't believe a word of it. "Mrs. Wentland, I hate to run, but I really do have some errands that are pressing. I suppose you could talk to Alec about these things, but I know what Lucy has already told him."

Her lips pressed together. "I'll do just that." She turned and headed toward the coffee shop.

I got into my car and slammed the door, gripping the steering wheel. It wasn't true, was it? The thought made me queasy. There was no way that Lucy was a killer. My best friend couldn't do something like that. But why had he ended up in her storage shed? It didn't make any sense.

I started the car, hesitating before I drove off. Did I go to Lucy's and ask her about it? I didn't want to seem confrontational, especially after the discussion we'd had the night before. I didn't want her to think that I didn't believe her because there was no way she had killed anyone, and I knew that. I started the car and headed toward Alec's office. He would know what to do, and I wanted him to know what Mrs. Wentland had said to me before she called him herself. What she said about Bruce talking to Lucy was shocking, but I couldn't imagine her lying about it. So had Bruce lied to her? I didn't know, but I was going to get to the bottom of it.

Chapter Thirteen

LUCY MADE EXCUSES TO not run with me three days in a row. I was starting to worry. Even though I didn't feel like running, I decided that I wasn't going to let my training slip. Lucy would come around. She always did. The sky was overcast, but it was warmer than I expected. After my run, I stopped by the Cup and Bean and picked up two mochas, then drove over to Alec's office. I had told him about what Mrs. Wentland had said a couple of days earlier, and in his usual calm manner, he said he would keep it in mind. I was hoping he had found out something new about the murder by now.

I almost slipped on the stairs on my way up to his office but caught myself in time and managed not to spill a drop of the mochas. I knocked with my shoe and then juggled the mochas, managing to open the office door. I grinned at Alec as he looked up from his computer screen.

"Greetings. I come bearing gifts." I held up the cups of coffee.

He grinned. "Well now, you've gone and made me happy."

"I knew it would cheer you up. And I'm going to make you even happier because I brought you one of the blueberry muffins I made last night." I leaned over the desk and kissed him, and then sat on the chair in front of his desk, setting the coffee down. I produced two blueberry muffins from my over-sized handbag and handed him one. "I actually brought it for Lucy, but I guess you're going to be the receiver of my gift instead."

One eyebrow shot up. "You mean I'm an afterthought?"

I shrugged. "I guess you're an afterthought today. Don't take offense, you're always number one on my list. Most of the time." I looked away and took a sip of my coffee. There were two more muffins in my handbag that I had intended to give to Lucy. They'd make a nice afternoon treat since she hadn't gone running with me.

He chuckled and picked up the muffin. "I love your blueberry muffins. They're one of the best things in life."

I smiled. "Oh, aren't you sweet?"

"That I am. Lucy still giving you the cold shoulder?"

I sighed. "Unfortunately, yes."

"She'll come around." He took a bite of the muffin and nodded appreciatively.

"I know. I just miss her. So tell me, how is everything going?" Worrying about Lucy would get me nowhere. Alec was right. She would come around, and I needed to know everything he knew about the case. He sometimes held out on me and didn't tell me everything, but this was different. This case involved my best friend. The same best friend that was giving me the cold shoulder.

He took another bite of his muffin and sat back in his chair, chewing thoughtfully. "I don't have a lot to go on just yet, but you know I'm working on things. I'm not going to stop until I find Bruce Wentland's killer."

I nodded. "I figured as much. But Lucy isn't speaking to me. Or rather, she will answer the phone when I call, but she makes excuses and won't go running with me in the mornings anymore."

One eyebrow shot up. "How long has this been going on?" Alec knew Lucy wasn't happy with me, but I hadn't told him everything until now.

I shrugged, looking down at the coffee in my hands. "I guess it's only been three days, but it's the three days after we had dinner and had our discussion with her about Bruce. I hate that she's holding this against me. It's not like we came out and said that we thought she was the killer. We know she isn't."

He nodded. "Lucy knows that you don't believe she's the killer. You know her too well. I know her too well. But we've got to get every bit of information we can so that I can find her ex-husband's killer. Certainly, she understands that."

I looked up at him. "I would think that she would. But I guess she got her feelings hurt when you asked her questions about her relationship with Bruce. Maybe I should go to her house and talk to her."

He thought about it for a moment and took a sip of his coffee. "Maybe you should give her a few more days? She's licking her wounds, and she probably needs some time to herself. She'll come around."

I shook my head. "There aren't any wounds to lick. We never accused her of anything."

"That's true, but I'm sure this murder hits too close to home for her. No joke intended. She's not unaware of how it must look to the police."

I sighed and rubbed my forehead. "Okay, I'll try to give her a little bit of space, but I really want to talk to her. I miss her."

He nodded. "She'll come around. Don't worry about it."

I was doing my best not to worry about it, but I couldn't stand that there was something between the two of us. "So what's going on with the case? Have you found out anything new? There's got to be someone somewhere that knows something about this. And I'm not talking about the killer. Killers can never shut their mouths, and they've probably let it slip by now."

He nodded. "You're right about that. They do tend to like to brag about what they've done, and I'm sure somebody will come forward soon."

I shook my head at him. "So you don't have anything new?" I hoped he was just holding out on me. The sooner the killer was arrested, the sooner Lucy and I could get back to normal.

"We're working on it, Allie. I promise we're going to get this thing sorted out. The only thing we've got that's new is that Bruce's RV was found outside of town. It had been burned, so we didn't find much. The lab will do some testing, and maybe we will have some answers soon."

I sat up. "Really? Do you think he was killed in his RV? Maybe they will find the killer's fingerprints in it."

He nodded and took a sip of his coffee. "We hope so. It wouldn't surprise me if he was killed in the RV, and they drove him to Lucy's shed in it. Time will tell."

This news made me a little more hopeful. "What do the police say? Have you talked to Yancey about this?"

"The police are scouring the area, questioning anybody we usually have on our radar when something goes down. And by the way, Sam went out on medical leave."

I looked at him with interest. "Really? What's wrong with him? Is it the pain in his behind?"

He looked at me quizzically. "Pain in his behind? What are you talking about?"

"Well, he's always been a pain in our behind. Especially mine. I figure if he's reaping what he sows, then he should have a pain in his behind."

He chuckled and shook his head. "You are something else, Allie. I don't know what's going on with him. Yancey said he wasn't at liberty to say, and I didn't want to press him. I didn't want him to feel like he had to give something away that he shouldn't."

"It is kind of odd, though," I said as I yawned. "Excuse me. I guess I didn't get enough sleep last night. But we haven't seen Sam in months, and he's always got his nose in our business."

He nodded. "Let's just thank our lucky stars that we've got some space for a while."

"All right. That's exactly what I'm going to do," I said, grinning.

We were quiet for a moment as we ate our muffins and drank our coffee. I looked up at Alec. "Alec, tell me the truth. What do you think about this murder? Do you think there's any way that Lucy could have killed Bruce?" I hated to ask the question. It felt like such a betrayal.

He hesitated. "Is there a reason why you're asking? I thought we had it settled that there was no way she could have done this."

I nodded. "Yes. That's right. But there are so many unanswered questions right now, and I want to hear from you that you aren't suspicious of her."

He took another sip of his coffee and set the cup down. He was quiet for a moment. "If it were anyone else, I would be suspicious. Very suspicious. But it's Lucy, and we both know her well enough to know that she couldn't have done this. But that doesn't mean that other people don't have their eye on her."

I tilted my head. "Yancey?"

He nodded. "He's highly suspicious of her. He really wants us to go after her. Let's keep this between the two of us."

His words chilled me to the bone. "I guess it's good that Sam Bailey isn't hanging around then. He would make life a lot more miserable for Lucy than Yancey would."

He sighed. "You can say that again. I'll just keep working on the case. Give Lucy a couple of days, and then go talk to her. I'm sure she's scared. It doesn't look good for her."

I nodded. "If it were me, I would be freaking out."

"As I recall, when I questioned you about a murder a couple of years ago, you were freaking out." He smirked.

I shook my head, got to my feet, and picked up my coffee. "I don't like to talk about the past. I'll see you this evening." I leaned over and gave him a quick kiss.

"See you."

I headed out the door and down the stairs. I couldn't stand not speaking to Lucy. We needed to clear her name as quickly as we could so things would get back to normal.

Chapter Fourteen

I DROVE HOME AND PARKED in the driveway. I couldn't get Lucy off my mind. Alec had wanted me to wait a few days before going to speak to her, but I needed to see her now. I drank the rest of my mocha while trying to talk myself out of it. It didn't work, so I backed out of my driveway and headed to the Cup and Bean for a fresh coffee for myself and one for Lucy. I still had two blueberry muffins with me, and I hoped that would butter her up.

Lucy looked surprised to see me when she answered the door.

I smiled. "Good morning, Lucy. I sure missed you on my run this morning. Are you feeling all right?" I held a coffee in each hand. I was sure that would be enough to get me through the door.

She nodded but ignored the coffee. This might be harder than I thought. "I guess I've been feeling a little under the weather. I think maybe I have a cold coming on."

"Oh, I'm sorry. I hate being sick. But I brought you coffee and a blueberry muffin to help your body mend. There's nothing like caffeine to heal your body, you know." I tried my best-friend smile on her, hoping to break the ice.

She tried to stifle a smile. "Oh? My doctor never mentioned that I should drink plenty of coffee when I get sick."

I shrugged. "Some doctors don't know much. Can I come in?"

She hesitated, then nodded. "Sure. Come in." I followed her into the house, and we headed to the kitchen table. I pulled the blueberry muffins from my purse and set them on the table. "I made these last night. Alec thinks they're the best blueberry muffins I've ever made."

She eyed them. They had a streusel topping on them and were filled with fresh, plump blueberries. "They do look tasty. I heard blueberries are good for your immune system."

I grinned. "Exactly. And I took the liberty of ordering you a mocha. I hope that's what you wanted." I handed a coffee and a muffin across the table to her.

"You bet. Anything with chocolate," she said, pulling the chair out and sitting down.

I sat down across from her. I wasn't sure where to go from here. I didn't want to pry, but at the same time, I needed my best friend in my life again. "So, Lucy, how have you been?"

She looked up at me as she peeled the paper liner from the blueberry muffin. "Oh, I guess I've been better. Finding my ex-husband dead in my storage shed wasn't the best day of my life. And I'm sure people must be talking about me."

Ouch. I guess I had that coming. "No, it wasn't a good day. But you know that Alec is doing everything he can to find Bruce's killer. I know he's going to find them soon."

She looked at me, one eyebrow raised. "Oh? You don't think that it was me who killed him?"

The question stung a little. "Lucy, neither Alec nor I believe that you could have had anything to do with Bruce's murder. You're not that kind of person. And besides that, if you had killed him, why would you lead me to his body? That doesn't even make sense." Forget about what Mrs. Wentland said about it. Lucy didn't do it.

She softened and nodded. "That's true. That would be a stupid move. I may be blond, but it's not natural. If I had done it, I would have dumped him in the ocean or the woods. But I didn't do it."

I nodded. "Of course not. But you don't have any idea who may have done it?" I was going out on a limb on that one.

She shook her head and took a bite of the muffin. "This is delicious. But like I said before, I don't know what was going on in Bruce's life these past several decades. We didn't stay in touch. When our marriage was over, it was over, and I was glad."

"I'm sure that it was difficult to be married to someone you didn't love." I looked at her as I said it.

She looked at me. "That's what it was, you know. I didn't love him. I was a kid just out of high school, and the idea of getting married was exciting. I had the white dress, and the flowers and my friends from school were my bridesmaids. I was so wrapped up in the ceremony that I didn't stop to think about whether I really and truly loved him. About six months into the marriage, I realized what a terrible mistake I had made. We were nothing alike, and his drinking was getting worse, and I didn't even care for Bruce much by that time, let alone love him."

I nodded. "That must have been a difficult position to be in."

She looked down at her coffee cup. "It was terrifying. Not only did I have to admit to myself that I'd made a terrible mistake, but I had to admit it to Bruce and to my parents." She looked at me now, and her eyes were sad. "They put out a lot of money on the wedding, and now I was going to have to tell them that it was all a waste because I didn't want to stay with Bruce. I did try to stick it out for another three or four months, but we were both miserable. In the end, it was better that we parted."

I'd never thought about being in a position like this, and I could see how hard it must have been, especially since she was so young. "I'm sorry that you went through that."

She sighed and picked up her cup of coffee. "I tell you, it was quite a learning experience. When Ed came along, I knew he was the right one for me, but I didn't want to commit to him. I didn't want to make the same mistake twice."

"How did you get past that?" I asked and took a sip of my coffee.

"I finally had to just decide to take the plunge. We ran down to the justice of the peace and got married. It didn't cost much, and I didn't have to drag my parents into it." She shrugged. "I've always felt guilty about that fancy wedding. My mother wanted me to be happy and spared no expense."

I reached across the table and patted her hand. "I'm sure she was glad once you found happiness with Ed."

She nodded. "The trouble is I wish I had had the big wedding with the white dress when I married Ed, so I would have had those memories with him. Instead, I had it with the wrong person."

"Oh, I'm sorry."

She shrugged again. "Live and learn."

I nodded. "I still can't imagine how Bruce ended up in your storage shed."

She shook her head. "Somebody wants to set me up. But there is something that I didn't tell you or Alec."

My heart sank a little. "What's that?"

"When I said that I'd only seen him across the beach about six months ago, that wasn't completely true. I ran into him at the grocery store about four months ago."

I tried to remain neutral at this information. Why wouldn't she have told us this from the beginning? "Oh? You talked to him?"

She nodded. "Yes, I didn't want to, but I almost ran right into him as I came around the corner of the cereal aisle. He acted happy to see me, but I was just stunned to be face-to-face with him."

"Did he say anything interesting?" I asked, leaning forward.

She nodded. "Yes. He said that he could hardly stand his wife, Peggy. Said they were having troubles. I didn't know why he was opening up to me and telling me that sort of thing. We were talking about us being crazy kids, and then all of a sudden, he's talking about his wife. I don't know if it meant anything or not, but the more I think about it, the more I think that maybe it did. Maybe his wife killed him, and she dragged him into my storage shed so that it would be blamed on me."

"Do you know Peggy well?"

She nodded. "Not very well. She was two years ahead of me in school. When she got out of high school, she got pregnant, and in a small town like this, back then getting pregnant without being married was still kind of a scandal. I figure she married Bruce to make herself look better."

"Was she aware that you were still here in town?"

She nodded. "I figure when Bruce got home from the grocery store, he probably mentioned that he had run into me. Maybe she was already planning this, and she decided that would be a great way to get away with murder. She kills her husband and leaves him in his ex-wife's storage shed. Maybe she tries to build it up to the police that we were bitter after all these years or something. I don't know. There are crazier things that have happened."

"You said that he was happy to see you. How happy?"

She shrugged. "He was smiling and asking me about my life. Then he brought up memories of us being crazy kids. That's all."

I sighed. I hoped that this piece of information didn't get Lucy into more trouble than she was already in. She shouldn't have kept it back. She also didn't mention that Bruce had asked her out. Had he lied to his mother about it? If so, why?

Chapter Fifteen

LUCY AND I SAT WITH coffee and blueberry muffins in front of us and laughed and talked, just like we always did. It felt good having her back in my life. Sure, it had only been three days that we weren't speaking, but it was a long three days.

"The sun has been out a lot lately, and it sure has been nice," Lucy said, gazing out her kitchen window. "And look at me, all this beautiful weather, and I missed out on three days of training. How are we ever going to run a half marathon if I don't show up every day?"

I nodded. "That's all right. We still have plenty of time to train, and I tend to do the same thing from time to time. But just you wait, we're going to get our training in, and we're going to make a good showing at the half marathon." I could hardly wait to run the half marathon with Lucy. When I had run a full marathon with Alec, I had really kind of ran it by myself because Alec was a much better runner than I was. I had never run a marathon before, and I was so far behind him that once they said go, I didn't see him again until the race was over. With Lucy, we would be able to run side-by-side, and that would be a lot more fun than running it alone.

She took a sip of her coffee, made a face, and then drained the cup and set it back on the table. "The Cup and Bean makes a great cup of coffee. I don't know why I can't get the hang of it here at home."

We were on our second cup of coffee, and she was right about that. "I'm not any better at making coffee. Alec has a smoother touch, so I just let him do it," I said, gazing out the kitchen window again. "Say, Lucy, have you gone back out to your storage shed? Maybe just to take a look around?" I wasn't sure I should bring it up, but I had been wondering about it.

Her eyes got bigger. "Not me. All I can think about is Bruce laying there face up with a knife in his chest." She shivered. "I don't know if I'll ever go back inside that shed again. Ed had to put the Christmas totes away for me after the police removed the crime scene tape."

I nodded. "I guess I can't blame you. I'd hate to think about a dead guy every time I went into my storage shed."

She nodded and leaned forward. "And what if he's still hanging around?" she whispered.

My brow furrowed. "What do you mean? What if he's still hanging around? They took his body to the morgue."

She shook her head. "That's not what I mean," she whispered again. "What if his ghost is still out there?"

I stared at her, my coffee cup in my hand. "You can't be serious." Since when did Lucy believe in ghosts?

She nodded. "Of course I am. We're talking about my ex-husband. He was a jerk. I could just see him hanging out in my storage shed, waiting for me to go out there to get something, and him jumping out and scaring me."

I'd laughed. "That would be kind of funny."

She shook her head. "It wouldn't be funny! There'd be nothing funny about that at all. I bet if it was your ex-husband, you'd be thinking twice about going out into the storage shed, too."

I laughed harder. "Lucy, your imagination has gotten away from you. There's nothing out in that shed besides the things that you've been storing out there."

She shrugged. "I certainly hope that's all that's out there. But just to be sure, I'm sending Ed out there from here on out."

I took a sip of coffee. "Seriously? You'll never go back into that shed?"

She shook her head. "Nope. That's Ed's job now. Honestly, I've been thinking that maybe we should just sell this house and find another."

I chuckled. "You come to my house, and you know that a body was found there. You were with me when we found it. Why don't you have any problem with that?"

She shook her head again. "Allie, I didn't even know that girl. But I knew Bruce. And I know exactly what he's capable of. He's going to hang out here in the afterlife."

I chuckled again and looked out the kitchen window. "Why don't we take a walk out into your backyard?"

Her eyes widened. "Haven't you heard a thing I said? I don't want to run into Bruce."

I grinned at her. "But what if the police overlooked something? The sun has been shining for more than a week, and the snow is melting. You can even see some of your old dead grass poking out of the snow in the back there. I wonder if something that was hidden in the snow could be visible now?" I looked at her, one eyebrow raised.

She hesitated, thinking this over. "I have to admit, that's a good idea. But I'm not going inside the shed. You hear me?"

I chuckled and got to my feet. "I'll go inside the shed for you. If Bruce tries to make a move on me, I'll give him a karate chop to his ghostly neck."

"Ha ha," she said sarcastically as she followed me through her kitchen door and out into the backyard. "You think you're being funny, but I'm serious about this. I think he might be hanging around. The other night I heard a scratching on our bedroom window in the middle of the night."

I looked at her. "You mean the night the wind was blowing?"

She nodded. "That was the night."

I glanced over at her bedroom window and pointed to the rosebush that was growing in front of it. "Call me a nonbeliever, but I would have to bet the wind was causing that rosebush to scratch against the window."

She sighed and rolled her eyes. "Sure, but it was probably scratching against the window because Bruce was making it happen and not the wind."

I chuckled, and we headed over to the storage shed. The padlock was secured on it, and it was a bright and shiny silver one. "You got a new lock?"

She nodded. "I wanted a nice, secure lock on it."

I nodded absently and walked around the front of the storage shed. The snow had melted, and the ground in front of it was muddy. I wasn't sure this would do us any good, but it didn't hurt to take a look. I ran the toe of my shoe across what was left of the snow in front of the shed door, but it just turned muddy.

Lucy gave the shed a wide berth as she walked around it and over to the side, near an oak tree. "I just can't imagine why somebody would bring him over here, other than to frame me. But why frame me? What did I do to anybody?"

I turned and looked at her. "Well, I hate to point out the obvious, but you are a bit of a smart-aleck with some people."

She snorted. "That's the pot calling the kettle black."

My eyes widened. "Whaaa—."

She shrugged. "Maybe I do have a smart-aleck attitude, but that still doesn't warrant somebody committing murder and then setting me up."

She was right. What on earth could somebody have against her that would make them kill somebody and then make it look like she had done it? We walked around to the back of the shed. There was a small gap between it and the fence, but of course, there was nothing back there. I sighed. The snow back here was packed tightly between the fence and the shed because it hadn't seen as much sun as the rest of the yard. I came back around the side of the shed and glanced over at the gate. They didn't keep a padlock on it, so it wouldn't have been hard for the killer to get in and out. I headed over and took a quick look, but didn't see anything. Darn. We needed a break in this case. I walked slowly back toward the shed, my eyes on the ground as I went. And then I saw it. I hurried over and knelt, picking up something white off the ground.

"What is it? Did you find something?" Lucy asked from the far side of the shed. I turned the object over in my hand. It was a white plastic bead with a hole through the center. I looked at her.

"A bead?" I held it up between my thumb and forefinger.

She shook her head and came over to look at it. "I wonder where it came from?"

"You don't recognize it?" I asked.

She shook her head again. "No, it's a kind of generic-looking bead, if you ask me. It doesn't seem familiar."

"You don't have any costume jewelry that it could have come off?" I asked, looking at her.

She squinted at it and then looked at me again. "Have you ever seen me wear cheap plastic costume jewelry?"

She had a point. I couldn't recall her ever wearing something that would have a bead this cheap looking. Unless it was part of a Halloween costume. "What about for a costume? Could it have been a part of a costume?"

She shook her head. "No. Not that I recall, anyway. Do you think it's something?"

"I don't know, but I'll take it to Alec and see what he has to say about it." If the darn thing weren't so generic-looking, I would get more excited about it. But this thing seriously could have come off anything. "What about a Christmas ornament? Do you have any Christmas ornaments that might have a bead like this?"

She shook her head. "I can't think of anything that would have a white plastic bead like that."

I nodded and tucked it into my coat pocket. "All right, it probably doesn't mean a thing, but I'll give it to Alec and see what he has to say about it."

"Well, make sure you point out to him that I don't wear cheap plastic costume jewelry. Under no circumstances would I do that. So not only do we have a killer, but we have someone who dresses poorly," she said.

I nodded. "Noted."

We headed back into the house to continue catching up. It would be great if the bead came off of something the killer had worn, but I didn't think it was going to be of much use.

Chapter Sixteen

I WAS JUST PUTTING on my coat and getting ready to leave Lucy's house when there was a knock at the door.

"I guess I better get that," Lucy said. "Ed probably forgot his key again. I swear that man can barely keep his head on his shoulders most days."

I chuckled. "Poor Ed."

When Lucy opened the door, Yancey Tucker and two other officers were standing on the front step. I'd be a liar if I said my heart didn't skip a beat.

"Well, good morning, Yancey, officers," Lucy said amicably. "What can I do for you, gentlemen?"

Yancey's eyes darted to me and then back to Lucy. He sighed and then straightened up. "Lucy Gray, I have a warrant for your arrest."

I was stunned. And I knew that if I was stunned, then Lucy was in complete shock.

"Yancey, what are you talking about?" I said as I hurried to Lucy's side.

"Yeah, Yancey," Lucy said breathlessly. "What are you talking about? A warrant for my arrest for what?"

Yancey nodded but made no move to arrest her. "Lucy, you know what I'm arresting you for. For the murder of Bruce Wentland."

"Yancey, you know that's ridiculous," I said, putting my hands on my hips. "Lucy could never kill anybody. There's no way, and you know it."

He turned to me. "Allie, this isn't any of your business. I don't mean to sound harsh when I say that, but I've got business with Lucy right now."

"Yancey, you don't believe for a minute that I killed anyone, do you?" Lucy stood up straight.

He turned back to Lucy. "I'm just doing my job, Lucy."

"It is not your job to arrest innocent people," I said. I knew I should keep my nose out of it, but I couldn't help myself. This was my best friend, and he was not taking her to jail. At least, not if I could help it.

Yancey ignored me. "I have a warrant for your arrest," he repeated to Lucy.

Lucy shook her head. "Yancey, I didn't do anything. You know I didn't. I couldn't kill anybody."

Yancey sighed. He was in a tough spot. Yancey and Lucy had gone to school together, and I knew in his heart that he knew there was no way Lucy could have killed anyone. The other two officers had their eyes on Lucy but remained silent. I reached into my coat pocket and pulled my cell phone out and hit send under Alec's number. He answered on the first ring. "Alec, Yancey's here trying to arrest Lucy. Did you know about this?"

There was silence. "No, I didn't know about it."

"Well, you better get down here and talk some sense into Yancey." I could feel my anger rising. This was ridiculous.

"I'll be right there," he said, and the line went dead.

"Yancey, Alec is coming down here right now. You're not going to arrest Lucy."

The two officers behind him stepped up onto the porch. "Allie, you know that we're just doing our jobs," Officer Tony Johnson said. "If you try to get in the middle of this, you may be taking a trip downtown yourself."

I narrowed my eyes at Tony, but I wasn't worried about it. Alec would get me out somehow. He would pull strings for me somehow.

"This isn't going to happen," I said. "Alec is on his way to straighten you out, and you will need to back up. Right now." I sounded strong, but I was a bowl of jelly on the inside. Alec needed to hurry.

Yancey sighed tiredly. "Allie, do I need to put you in handcuffs first? Is that the only way we're going to be able to arrest Lucy?"

And suddenly I didn't feel so sure of myself anymore. I glanced over at Lucy, and her eyes were wide. "Yancey, isn't there something else that can be done? It doesn't have to be done this way, does it?"

"I'm afraid it does."

"Can I call Ed? I need to call Ed," Lucy said, turning around and hunting for her purse.

"Lucy, you need to come right back here," Yancey said, stepping inside the house. "Don't make me come after you."

Lucy seemed dazed as she hunted for her purse. "My phone is in my purse. I'm sure it is. I can't find it, Allie. I need to call Ed."

"You can call Ed from the jail," Yancey said as he strode across the living room to where Lucy was hunting behind the couch cushions for her purse. "Lucy, I don't want to do this, but I have to. I need you to put your hands behind your head."

Lucy's eyes widened. "Yancey, I am not a murderer. I am not a criminal of any kind. And I need Ed. I need Ed right now."

"As I said, you can call him from the jail. But I have to arrest you now. Please don't make this any harder than it has to be."

Lucy swallowed and slowly put her hands behind her head. My heart sank, and I felt like crying. Nobody in this room thought that Lucy could've hurt anybody, let alone murder someone. And yet, she was being arrested for murder.

Yancey began reading Lucy her rights, and then he put the handcuffs on her. He saved her the humiliation of patting her down. It may have gone against police protocol, but there was no way Lucy was going to hurt anyone, and he knew it.

"Don't worry, Lucy, we will find a way to get you out. We all know that you're innocent," I said as Yancey led her past me.

The other two officers stepped back as Yancey and Lucy passed, and they followed them out to the squad cars. I stood on the doorstep and swallowed back the lump in my throat. "I'll lock up the house, and I'll find Ed. I'll track him down, and we will be at the police station very soon," I called to her before she got into the squad car.

My heart felt like it was going to explode. This was wrong. They had no right to do this. As they pulled away, Alec pulled up and parked in front of the house. He got out and glanced in the direction of the police cars as they pulled away and then looked back at me.

"They took her, Alec! They arrested her! We need to find Ed!" I was beside myself at this point.

He hurried over to me. "We'll find Ed, and then we'll head down to the police station."

I nodded, and we went inside the house and hunted for Lucy's purse. She would need what was in there, I was sure. Whether they would let her have it or not, I didn't know, but I was sure that she needed it. A woman needs her purse.

"This is ridiculous," I said when I finally found it in her bedroom. "I can't believe that it's gotten to this point. I can't believe that anyone would think that she had done such a thing. We need to get her out. And why didn't anyone tell you about this?"

He nodded. "I suppose they thought I might interfere. We'll do everything we can to get her out. Let's find Ed so we can get down to the police station."

I crossed my arms in front of myself, wanting to scream, but holding it back. "This is ridiculous. I can't believe Lucy was arrested. Did you ever find out if the police were really called on Bruce and his stepson fighting? Craig sure acted like they had this great relationship."

He placed his hands on my crossed arms. "It's going to be okay. Trust me. But in answer to your question, the police were called out, but things had settled down by the time they got there. Bruce and Craig insisted there had to be some kind of mistake."

I sighed. "Yeah, I bet there was. If you ask me, there's something fishy there."

"I don't doubt it. I'm going to go down to the station and see what I can find out. I'll see if I can get ahold of Ed." He kissed me and then left.

I sighed. Lucy had to be frantic by now. The thought of going to jail gave me shivers. Getting her out was going to be tricky, but we'd do it.

Chapter Seventeen

I LOCKED UP LUCY'S house and went out to my car. Lucy was the sort of person who didn't show her emotions often, but I knew that this had her terribly upset. I had to do something to help her. I just wasn't sure what.

The only person that could have killed Bruce was his wife. It made sense, didn't it? If what Bruce's mother said was true, that he still had a thing for Lucy after they had gotten divorced, then it had to be his wife that killed him. And how easy would it have been to set Lucy up? They never locked the shed, and there wasn't a padlock on their back gate. Leaving Bruce's body in Lucy's shed would make the police look at her, and not Peggy.

I drove over to Peggy's house and strode up the walk. That woman was going to pay for what she did to my friend. I pounded on the door harder than I intended, and when no one answered, I repeated it. Finally, after what seemed like forever, Peggy opened the door. She looked surprised to see me.

"Allie, can I help you with something?"

I breathed out. "You bet you can help me. You can tell the police that you killed your husband."

Her eyes got big, and she shook her head. "What are you talking about? Tell the police that I killed my husband? Have you lost your mind? I would never kill my husband." She had an old blue apron on that was stained. I wanted to say something snotty about it, but that would take us off track.

"You know what I'm talking about. You killed Bruce and framed Lucy."

She frowned. "I think you've lost your mind. If you'll excuse me, I've got work to do."

"Oh, come on, Peggy, you know what you did. You've always been jealous of Lucy, haven't you? Why did you move back to Sandy Harbor? Why couldn't you stay where you were? Everybody would have been happy that way." This was starting wrong, but it was like I was running downhill, and every time I opened my mouth, the faster I rolled down the hill.

Her brow furrowed. "Allie, I believe you've lost your mind. What on earth are you talking about?"

"Just what I said. You killed Bruce, and you framed Lucy. You need to go down to the police station and confess what you did." I suddenly had the desire to slap the smirk off her face.

She laughed. "Really, Allie, you've lost your mind. How stupid do you think the police are? Bruce's body was found in Lucy's storage shed. Of course, they're going to come looking for her. She killed him because she never got over him. How stupid was she, though, to just leave him there in her shed? That's what I don't get. Why do that when the police would eventually find him there?"

I hate being laughed at. "Listen, Peggy, I'm not fooling around now. You need to confess to what you did."

She rolled her eyes. "Honestly, Allie, I've got things to do. If you'll excuse me." I stuck my foot in the door, and she turned red. "What are you doing?"

"I'm not playing games with you, Peggy. We all know the truth, and it's time you confessed."

"I suggest that you get your foot out of my door before I break it. Go on and get out of here. I don't have time for this."

This was getting me nowhere, and I didn't relish the thought of a broken foot. "Peggy, you've got to do the right thing. You've got to tell the police what you did." I was starting to feel desperate. It's not like I could wring her neck and force the truth out of her. Although I wanted to.

"I'm calling the police." She tried to slam the door, but my foot was still there, so she turned around and hurried inside.

I knew I shouldn't do it, but I followed her in. "Peggy, just tell the truth. Confession is good for the soul."

She looked over her shoulder, shocked that I had followed her inside the house. She grabbed her purse from an end table and started rummaging through it. "Get out of here, Allie. I'm sure you won't enjoy doing time for breaking and entering."

"I didn't break or enter. You opened the door, and I just walked through it."

"Trespassing then. I certainly did not permit you to come into my house." She pulled her phone from her purse and held it up to me. "I'm calling the police."

"No, don't call the police," I relented. Alec wouldn't appreciate needing to bail me out. "Peggy, I just want your husband's killer found. That's all I want."

She studied me for a moment, her cell phone still clutched in her hand. "Oh yeah? Well, I do know who did it. It was Lucy and Darrell Peters."

"What on earth are you talking about?" I couldn't imagine why she would think that Lucy and Darrell Peters would get together and kill Bruce.

She laughed. "Don't tell me. Your best friend didn't tell you what was going on?"

I shook my head slowly. Lately, there had been more things that Lucy hadn't told me about than I cared to admit. Was there something else? "I don't know what you're talking about. You're just stalling."

"Of course, you don't. After Bruce and Lucy broke up, she dated Darrell." She smiled smugly.

I gasped. I couldn't help myself. "What are you talking about?"

She laughed again. Now I really wanted to slap her. "Lucy and Darrell were fooling around before she divorced Bruce. You don't know anything about your best friend, do you? As I said, the two of them were fooling around together. Bruce had suspected it while they were still married, but he could never get either of them to admit it."

She was lying. Of course she was. Lucy would have told me about it. "Then why would Bruce go into business with Darrell if he was so certain he and Lucy were seeing each other?"

She hesitated, and if I wasn't mistaken, I thought I saw a bit of doubt in her eyes. "Because Darrell finally admitted to it, but he swore that it was after they had gotten divorced. He swore that Lucy had been coming around and hinting to him that she wanted him to ask her out, and so he did. Supposedly, she and Bruce were already divorced, so he agreed."

"You're not making any sense. A minute ago you said that they were fooling around while Bruce and Lucy were married. Now you're saying that it was after they had gotten divorced." I crossed my arms in front of myself. I smelled a rat and a liar.

She nodded. "Do you think I'm stupid? Just because Bruce believed that they didn't fool around until after they got divorced doesn't mean that I do. I know the two of them were together. I never liked Darrell, he's so full of himself. He always tried to take credit for any success the business had. I told Bruce years ago to get rid of him, but they had been friends since they were kids, and he just couldn't bring himself to do it."

I was trying to make sense of the things that she was saying. How much of it was true? If she was her husband's killer, then probably none of it. But I didn't know that for sure.

"Do you have proof that they were seeing each other before Lucy and Bruce were divorced?"

She shrugged. "Two of my friends said they saw them together before the divorce."

I didn't know what to think about all of this. "If Bruce and Darrell were such good, lifelong friends, then why were they breaking up the business partnership?" There. I had her.

She snorted. "The business wasn't doing that great. Not that that's any of your business. Now get out of my house. I'm calling the police."

"No, you're not. Because you're the killer. And you don't want them to take a closer look at you."

She shook her head and rolled her eyes, dialing 911. I groaned. The last thing I needed was to go to jail. But then, maybe they would put Lucy and me in the same jail cell, and we could keep each other company. I shook the thought away as Peggy waited for the operator to answer.

"You don't need to call the police. I'm leaving." The operator had apparently come on the line because she began telling them my name and the fact that I had forced my way into the house. "You're such a liar, Peggy. You're lying about this and you're lying about killing your husband, too," I said over my shoulder as I hurried out the door.

I got into my car and started it. Alec would have a fit if he found out that I was arrested. I sped away, wondering if the police would come to my door or if I should go someplace else until I could talk to Alec and tell him what happened.

Chapter Eighteen

WHAT PEGGY HAD SAID took some nerve. Claiming that Lucy had killed Bruce was just ridiculous. But even I had to admit that Lucy had been holding back an awful lot of information ever since we'd found her ex-husband's body. First, she hadn't told me that she had been married before, and then she conveniently forgot to mention she had spoken to Bruce since he had returned to Sandy Harbor, and now Peggy was saying that she had dated Darrell Peters before she was divorced from Bruce. It was a long time ago, so maybe it wasn't that big of a deal back then. Except that it was now. Why hadn't she just told me about all of it? What was the point of keeping it to herself? She knew that Alec needed all the information he could get to find Bruce's killer.

When I got home, I sat on the couch and put my feet up on the coffee table, and sighed. My black cat, Dixie, came and sat on my lap, looking up at me and purring.

I smiled and ran a hand over his head. "You're not going to believe this, Dixie, but human stuff is aggravating."

As if he understood, he leaned forward, and his tongue darted out, licking my neck. His purring amplified, and he closed his eyes. It was his way of comforting me.

"Okay, maybe you do understand. I bet you're so glad you're a cat. At this point, I wouldn't mind being one myself."

At least in his world, all you had to worry about was if your food bowl was filled and the litter box was empty. I put my head on the back of the couch and stared up at the ceiling. I hoped this situation wouldn't go on much longer. The sooner Bruce's killer was put behind bars, the better. Lucy was not that killer, and we needed to figure out a way to get her out of jail.

The front door opened, and I heard footsteps down the hall. "In here!"

Alec came to the doorway of the living room and stopped. "I hope I'm not interrupting anything."

I shook my head and looked at him. "Nope. Dixie and I were just hanging out. What's going on?"

He sighed tiredly and crossed the room.

"I don't like the sound of that."

He shook his head and sat down next to me, and laid his head on my shoulder as he ran a hand over Dixie's head. "No, I don't like the sound of it either. Poor Lucy is beside herself in that jail."

I looked at him. "Wait a minute. Why is she still there? Why isn't she at least out on bail?"

He shook his head. "A judge has to set bail."

I swallowed. "So that means Lucy is staying the night?"

He nodded. "She's staying the night. And maybe longer, depending on how quickly they can get around to setting bail."

The thought made me queasy. I didn't think I would last long in jail. "Isn't there anything you can do?"

He shook his head. "No. Other than trying to find Bruce's killer, there's not a lot I can do. Yancey isn't about to bend rules just because he's a friend of mine. I don't blame him. This is serious business."

"I knew you'd say that." I sighed and put my head on the back of the couch again. Poor Lucy. Poor Ed. Sometimes they acted like they didn't get along well, but I knew the truth was that the two were stuck to each other like glue. This was going to be devastating for both of them.

"Did you talk to Ed?" I asked.

He nodded. "Yeah, I called him, and we talked when he came down. Poor guy. I don't think he ever thought it would come to this. He didn't say as much, but he's worried."

I shook my head. "I don't think any of us thought it would come to this."

Alec's phone rang, and he dug into his coat pocket and pulled it out. "It's Yancey." He answered it and then listened for a few moments. "I see. This is all very strange. I see."

I sat up at the word strange. Was it strange enough to get my friend out of jail?

He said yes a few more times, and then he hung up and turned to me. "You're not going to believe what just happened."

"At this point, I'll believe anything." I still hadn't had the chance to tell him about Lucy's dating Darrell, possibly while she was still married to Bruce, and I hoped that this wasn't the news Yancey had given him. It would only condemn her more.

"Peggy Wentland showed up at the police station and said that her son killed Bruce."

My mouth dropped open as my brain tried to comprehend what he was telling me. "Are you sure about that?"

He grinned. "Yes, I'm sure about it. I just got off the phone with Yancey."

I shook my head slowly, trying to take this in. "But I just saw her less than an hour ago, and she swore up and down that it was Lucy that did it. She said Lucy had dated Darrel Peters before she and Bruce were divorced. But of course, Lucy never mentioned it. Peggy swore it was proof that she killed him."

He shrugged. "She's at the police station right now, giving them her statement."

I sat back on the couch. "Why? Why would she throw her son under the bus? Especially when everything looks so bad for Lucy?"

He shook his head. "I don't know. It does sound suspicious."

I turned and looked at him. "What do you want to bet that her reason is that she actually did the killing, but she's trying to get her son to pay for it?"

He nodded. "Wouldn't surprise me a bit. This thing gets crazier by the minute. So Lucy didn't tell us the truth again?" he asked thoughtfully.

I scratched Dixie's ear. "Yeah, seems like she's getting good at that."

He turned to me, one eyebrow raised. "We'll have to have a talk with her about that."

I sighed. "Maybe she was scared to tell us everything. She may have thought it would incriminate her more."

"It incriminates her more to keep the truth from the police when it's found out later. She would have been better off telling everything she knew."

I sighed. He was right, of course. "Wait a minute, so if Peggy's pointing the finger at her son, are they going to let Lucy out?"

"Not yet. Yancey just wanted to give me a call and give me a heads up. He sounded like he was shocked about it too."

"Okay, so why are they going to keep Lucy?"

"They're going to have to look into Peggy's story. You know how it is."

I nodded. "They need to let Lucy go. They have absolutely no proof that she did anything."

He looked at me, his eyebrow raised again. "Oh really? They had no proof?"

"Okay, fine, his dead body was found in her storage shed. And a bunch of fingerprints that belonged to her were all over the shed. But who else would they belong to besides her and Ed? I don't count the fingerprints as evidence."

"No, neither does anyone else. But since he was dead in her shed and he's her ex, that pretty much tied it all up."

I shook my head. "It's not enough. If they can get a confession out of Craig Foster, they've got to let Lucy go then, right?"

"Yes. But we'll have to wait until they can get that confession."

I looked at him. "Why do we need to wait? Aren't they going to haul him in and shine a bright light into his eyes? Make him sign a confession?"

He chuckled. "Everything takes time. I seriously doubt that Craig is going to be thrilled that his mother threw him under the bus, and he isn't going to just confess everything without some pressure."

He was right, of course. I knew that. I was just worried about Lucy. I put Dixie in Alec's lap and got to my feet.

"Where are you going?"

"I'm going to make Lucy some lemon poppy seed muffins. They're one of her favorites, and I'm sure she'll appreciate it when she gets out."

"Well, I know I will," he said, stroking Dixie's head.

"They're for Lucy."

I heard a sigh as I left the room.

Chapter Nineteen

ALEC LEFT FOR THE POLICE station early the next morning, and after sitting patiently beside my phone and not getting a call back from him, I decided to see what was going on. I'd whipped up a fresh batch of my blueberry streusel muffins, so I boxed them up and jumped in my car, and drove down there. I hoped Lucy would be released today. I yawned. Hopefully, she had slept better than I had, but I doubted it.

Alec was exiting the station as I pulled into a parking space. I grinned and jumped out of the car. "Well, fancy seeing you here, stranger."

The look on his face said he was puzzled to see me here. "What do you mean, fancy meeting you here? I told you I was going to be here all day. What are you doing here?"

I ran around to the passenger side of my car and removed the box of blueberry muffins, shutting the door with my hip. "Of course, silly. I know that. But I decided that I had better come and check up on you and see what's going on. Plus, I brought muffins for the team." I held the box up to him so he could get a better look at it.

He shook his head. "Allie, what team? What are you talking about?"

I frowned. "Oh, come on, Alec. You know that the officers here are on our team. You've been hired to catch a killer, and they are assisting."

He sighed and rolled his eyes. "Allie, we are assisting them, not the other way around. Don't let anybody hear you saying otherwise, or we may not get any future work from them."

I shrugged with the box still in hand. "I'm not going to say a word. So what's going on? Why are you leaving? Did he confess?" I hurried closer to him.

"No, he won't confess. We've been interviewing him all day, and he claims he had nothing to do with the murder."

That was not what I was expecting him to say. "Are you kidding me? Why would his mother throw him under the bus if he had nothing to do with the murder? I mean, mothers don't do that. Or at least, I wouldn't."

He smiled. "And you are a gem." He leaned over the box and kissed me. "Why don't you run inside with those muffins, and then I'll meet you back at the house?"

I narrowed my eyes at him. "When will you meet me back at the house?"

He shoved his hands into his coat pocket and jingled his keys. "Oh, I don't know, shortly I guess."

"Shortly? That's rather vague. Where are you headed? What are you doing?" I was suspicious that he was about to do something exciting, and he was going to leave me out of it.

"You sure are full of questions today. I've got another interview to do, and I will see you later this evening." He leaned over and kissed me again, and turned toward his car.

"Hold on, Sherlock, I'm not letting you run off and conduct an interview without me."

"I think you are. You've got to put those blueberry muffins in the break room, and by the time you're done with that, I will be halfway across town." He chuckled and pulled his car keys from his coat pocket, heading toward his car.

There was no way I was going to miss out on this. We were too close to figuring out who Bruce's killer was. I ran behind him and almost slipped and fell in the melting snow. "Woo! I'm coming with you." I hurried to the other side of his car, opened the passenger door, and got in before he had a chance to say anything.

Opening his door, he slid in behind the steering wheel. "You made those muffins for the team. Why don't you go hand them out to the team?" He eyed me.

I shook my head and set the box of muffins in the back seat. "There's plenty of time for that later. I want to know what you know."

He groaned and started the car. "You are the nosiest person I know."

"I know."

PEGGY'S DRAPES WERE drawn when we pulled up to her house. The walkway was free of snow thanks to all the sunshine we had been getting. We got out of the car and headed up to the front door. Alec leaned down toward me as we walked. "You should have brought those muffins. Maybe you could talk her into confessing."

I scowled. Alec was a smart aleck. But I hurried back to the car and grabbed the box of muffins anyway. There were two dozen sweet, moist blueberry muffins in this box, and if that didn't coax a confession out of someone, nothing would. I could make more muffins for the officers later.

Peggy looked surprised to see us when she answered the door. She narrowed her eyes at me.

"Peggy, how are you this afternoon?" Alec asked.

She sniffed. "I'm fine." Her tone said that she wasn't exactly fine. Actually. it sounded a bit terse.

"May we come in?" Alec asked politely.

She sighed. "Why? I've already told the police everything that I have to say. And she is not welcome."

"Peggy, I apologize for the misunderstanding yesterday. I don't know what I was thinking. I baked some fresh blueberry muffins for you to make up for it. I've been working on the streusel topping for them, and I think I may have gotten it just right. I don't suppose you could try one of them and let me know?"

Her eyes went to the box and then back to me. "I know you're just trying to get in the door with your baked goods. And then what will you do? Accuse me of murdering Jimmy Hoffa?"

I chuckled. "You caught me. I'm always doing crazy things like that. But I'm telling you, these blueberry muffins are worth a few minutes of your time. It may sound like I'm bragging, but I'm not. I promise."

Reluctantly, she stepped back and allowed us to enter. "I suppose we could have some coffee with those muffins," she said over her shoulder. We followed her into the kitchen. Peggy's kitchen was a bright, blue-accented affair. The porcelain tile on the backsplash had blue and white flowers, and her small appliances were a matching shade of blue.

"Coffee would be divine," I said and hurried over to the table and set the box down, opening it up. "I love your kitchen. It's so bright and cheery."

"I've already got a pot of coffee brewing, so it won't take long," she said, ignoring the comment. She got three coffee mugs from the cupboard and brought the coffee pot over to the table.

I nodded as she got the cream and sugar out of the refrigerator, and we took a seat.

"Those do look good," she said, eyeing the box of muffins. I had made them in an oversized muffin pan, and each one was not only large, but they were moist and filled with juicy blueberries.

"Wait until you try one," I said, pushing the box toward her. She reached in and pulled one out.

"They smell wonderful."

"Peggy, we talked with your son." Alec poured cream into his cup, keeping one eye on her.

Her eyes teared up, and she frowned. "I just can't imagine why he would kill Bruce. They were always so close. All I ever wanted was a father for my baby, and Bruce was the best." She began peeling the paper from the muffin. If she knew more than she was letting on, she had a great poker face.

Alec nodded and took one of the blueberry muffins. "He said that you killed him."

Peggy's eyes widened, and she stared at him. "Why would he say something like that? I can't believe he would say that. Are you sure he said that? That's just crazy. Bruce and I were happy together."

I was surprised that she was so stunned. She had pointed the finger at her son first. Wouldn't she expect him to accuse her right back?

Alec nodded as he continued to stir his coffee. "I'm absolutely certain. I was there in the room when he said it."

I took one of the blueberry muffins, watching Peggy. She still wasn't batting an eye, but the tension in the room went up a couple of notches. She took a bite of the muffin and groaned softly.

"Oh, Allie, this is the most perfectly delicious and moist blueberry muffin I've ever had. How do you do it?"

I smiled as I poured cream into my cup. "Butter. Lots and lots of butter. Not to mention a lot of pure vanilla extract. I love vanilla, and it accents so many other flavors so well." Were we really talking about baking in the middle of a conversation about her son accusing her of murder?

She nodded and took another bite. "Delectable. That's all I can say about this muffin. It is purely delectable."

I glanced at Alec, and he was watching her. He sat up straight. "So what about it, Peggy? Did you have something to do with your husband's murder?"

She shook her head. "No. I absolutely did not." She took a sip of her coffee and met Alec's gaze evenly.

I wasn't sure where we were going to go with this. She didn't look the least bit nervous or upset about what we were talking about. A lifetime behind bars should scare anyone, whether they were innocent or guilty.

"I'm not sure I believe you," Alec said flatly. "I think that you killed your husband. It makes sense, after all. The two of you were having issues, and he was going to divorce you."

At this, Peggy's eyes widened, and she reached for the white beaded necklace around her neck. She gave it a half-inch turn and shook her head. "That's ridiculous. We were happily married. Who told you that?"

"Your husband's business partner, Darrell Peters," Alec said. "Is it not true?"

She shook her head again and gave the necklace another turn. And that was when I saw it. She was wearing beaded chandelier earrings, the cheap plastic kind. I squinted. There was a white bead missing.

"I'm telling you, detective, I had nothing to do with my husband's death. We were happily married, and both of us were just thrilled to move back to Sandy Harbor. We had missed it so much." She took another bite of her muffin without looking at Alec.

He took a sip of his coffee. "Then why would Darrell say that?"

She waved a dismissive hand. "Oh, that Darrell. He drinks. A lot. I told Bruce that dissolving the partnership was the best idea he'd had in a long time."

"Oh Peggy, those are darling earrings you've got there. But it looks like you've lost a bead." I turned and looked at Alec. You wouldn't have noticed it had you not known Alec well, but I could see the excitement in his eyes.

"Will you look at that," Alec said. "You're missing a bead from your earring."

She hesitated and reached a hand up to it. "Oh? I didn't even notice it. My son bought me these when he was in the second grade. He saved his allowance, and his grandmother took him Mother's Day shopping." She chuckled, and if I wasn't mistaken, there was just a tinge of nervousness now. "I've held onto them for forever. It was such a sweet, thoughtful gift from my darling boy. I could never part with them, and now I have gone and lost a bead." She set the muffin down and removed the earring, laying it on the table.

"They certainly are adorable," I said. "I could just picture a seven-year-old picking those out for his mother for Mother's Day. I have a lot of adorable little gifts that my kids got me when they were younger, too, so I know what you mean about not parting with it." Of course, I could never turn one of my kids in for murder, either. Call me crazy.

She looked up at me and smiled. "There's nothing like a gift from your child when they've done their best to buy the thing that you like the most. I always wear earrings, and he wanted to get me something to add to my collection."

"It's funny," Alec said, letting the words trail off a moment. "We found a white bead that looks pretty much identical to the one that would fit right in that setting."

Peggy didn't look at us. She clutched the earring and got up from the table.

Chapter Twenty

I SAT BACK ON THE COUCH and yawned. "So they both did it."

Alec took a sip of his hot cocoa and nodded. "They both did it."

I shook my head. "I don't get it. Why? Why kill your husband? And your stepfather?"

He turned and looked at me. "Money."

"Oh, it's always the money, isn't it? I don't know why people get that way. It isn't worth killing somebody over." I took a sip of my hot cocoa. The sunny days had suddenly turned to overcast and then to snow again. A fire was roaring in the fireplace, and I was snuggled up next to Alec. It was late, and I was glad he was home.

"Don't ask me. I've never understood why anyone would be driven to the point of murder. Got any of those blueberry muffins left?"

I shook my head. "No, I left them all at Peggy's. I guess we can drive over there and see if there's any left?"

He laughed. "No one's home, and if they were, I seriously doubt anybody would give us those muffins back. And if somebody did, I don't think I would eat one."

"You've got a point," I said and took another sip of my cocoa. Dixie was lying on a pillow in front of the fireplace, sound asleep.

"You are going to make me more muffins, aren't you?"

I nodded and yawned again. "Yes, I'll make you some more. I'll even make the officers at the station some muffins."

"Good. Just don't give them all to them. And you might make some for Lucy and Ed. They've been through a lot these past couple of weeks."

I nodded. "Tell me about it. I still can't get over Peggy squealing on her own son like that. She acted like those earrings meant so much to her, but then she turns him in. You would think that a mother's instinct would be to protect her young. It certainly is for me."

"You would think so. I guess when you're facing a lifetime prison sentence, you have to make decisions."

I chuckled. "I guess when you put it that way, maybe I would throw Jennifer to the wolves."

"What about Thad?"

I shook my head. "No, he's my favorite. He's going to take care of me in my old age."

He laughed, almost choking on his cocoa. When he recovered, he wrapped his arms around me. "That's what I love about you. You're so practical."

"That I am. So why did she decide to go to the police and squeal on him? And why did she think he wouldn't tell the police she helped him? If she had kept her mouth shut, chances were good they would have gotten away with it."

"She thought Craig was her devoted son who would never squeal on her. But he wasn't crazy about a life sentence, either. And the reason she turned him in? It was you. She said she was worried because you were asking questions. Apparently Darrell Peters and Craig had told her you had been asking questions." He turned and looked at me.

I turned to him, surprised. "Well, in that case, I think I deserve the payment for this case."

His brow furrowed. "How do you figure?"

I shrugged. "You just said that I caused her to turn her son in. We never would've gotten a confession if I wasn't so nosy." Finally, my nosiness was paying off.

He nodded. "You do have a point. But I'm not giving you any of the money."

I gasped in mock horror. "How dare you? Oh well. You can take me out for a nice meal someplace."

He looked at me, one eyebrow raised. "Stan's Crabshack?"

"Now you're talking," I said. "They've got the best seafood around, and I heard they've got an all-you-can-eat seafood bar now."

His eyes widened. "Really?"

I nodded. "I heard it from Hazel Taylor. I ran into her at the grocery store the other day when I was buying blueberries, and she said Stan's had set up a seafood bar. Poor Stan. He's going to go out of business, you know."

"I hope not," he said and took another sip of his cocoa. "None of the other seafood places up and down the coast are nearly as good as Stan's."

I nodded. "Yes, but after I partake of their all-you-can-eat seafood bar, they're going to end up going bankrupt. I can put some shrimp away, you know."

"I noticed that. I wasn't going to point it out, but I did notice."

I chuckled and leaned my head on his shoulder. I would never understand the ways of a killer. There had to be a better way to settle differences. Get a divorce. Move away. Anything other than murder. Peggy would have ended up getting a sizable chunk of his business if she would have divorced him. But instead, she killed him and prison wasn't going to be a comfortable place.

The End

Sign up to receive my newsletter for updates on new releases and sales:

https://www.subscribepage.com/kathleen-suzette

Follow me on Facebook:

https://www.facebook.com/Kathleen-Suzette-Kate-Bell-authors-759206390932120

Books by Kathleen Suzette:

A Lemon Creek Mystery
Murder at the Ranch
A Lemon Creek Mystery, book 1
The Art of Murder
A Lemon Creek Mystery, book 2

Body on the Boat
A Lemon Creek Mystery, book 3
A Rainey Daye Cozy Mystery Series
Clam Chowder and a Murder
A Rainey Daye Cozy Mystery, book 1
A Short Stack and a Murder
A Rainey Daye Cozy Mystery, book 2
Cherry Pie and a Murder
A Rainey Daye Cozy Mystery, book 3
Barbecue and a Murder
A Rainey Daye Cozy Mystery, book 4
Birthday Cake and a Murder
A Rainey Daye Cozy Mystery, book 5
Hot Cider and a Murder
A Rainey Daye Cozy Mystery, book 6
Roast Turkey and a Murder
A Rainey Daye Cozy Mystery, book 7
Gingerbread and a Murder
A Rainey Daye Cozy Mystery, book 8
Fish Fry and a Murder
A Rainey Daye Cozy Mystery, book 9
Cupcakes and a Murder
A Rainey Daye Cozy Mystery, book 10
Lemon Pie and a Murder
A Rainey Daye Cozy Mystery, book 11
Pasta and a Murder
A Rainey Daye Cozy Mystery, book 12
Chocolate Cake and a Murder
A Rainey Daye Cozy Mystery, book 13

Pumpkin Spice Donuts and a Murder
A Rainey Daye Cozy Mystery, book 14
A Pumpkin Hollow Mystery Series
Candy Coated Murder
A Pumpkin Hollow Mystery, book 1
Murderously Sweet
A Pumpkin Hollow Mystery, book 2
Chocolate Covered Murder
A Pumpkin Hollow Mystery, book 3
Death and Sweets
A Pumpkin Hollow Mystery, book 4
Sugared Demise
A Pumpkin Hollow Mystery, book 5
Confectionately Dead
A Pumpkin Hollow Mystery, book 6
Hard Candy and a Killer
A Pumpkin Hollow Mystery, book 7
Candy Kisses and a Killer
A Pumpkin Hollow Mystery, book 8
Terminal Taffy
A Pumpkin Hollow Mystery, book 9
Fudgy Fatality
A Pumpkin Hollow Mystery, book 10
Truffled Murder
A Pumpkin Hollow Mystery, book 11
Caramel Murder
A Pumpkin Hollow Mystery, book 12
Peppermint Fudge Killer
A Pumpkin Hollow Mystery, book 13

Chocolate Heart Killer
A Pumpkin Hollow Mystery, book 14
Strawberry Creams and Death
A Pumpkin Hollow Mystery, book 15
Pumpkin Spice Lies
A Pumpkin Hollow Mystery, book 16
Sweetly Dead
A Pumpkin Hollow Mystery, book 17
Deadly Valentine
A Pumpkin Hollow Mystery, book 18
Death and a Peppermint Patty
A Pumpkin Hollow Mystery, book 19
Sugar, Spice, and Murder
A Pumpkin Hollow Mystery, book 20
Candy Crushed
A Pumpkin Hollow Mystery, book 21
Trick or Treat
A Pumpkin Hollow Mystery, book 22

A Freshly Baked Cozy Mystery Series
Apple Pie a la Murder,
A Freshly Baked Cozy Mystery, Book 1
Trick or Treat and Murder,
A Freshly Baked Cozy Mystery, Book 2
Thankfully Dead
A Freshly Baked Cozy Mystery, Book 3
Candy Cane Killer
A Freshly Baked Cozy Mystery, Book 4
Ice Cold Murder
A Freshly Baked Cozy Mystery, Book 5

Love is Murder
A Freshly Baked Cozy Mystery, Book 6
Strawberry Surprise Killer
A Freshly Baked Cozy Mystery, Book 7
Plum Dead
A Freshly Baked Cozy Mystery, book 8
Red, White, and Blue Murder
A Freshly Baked Cozy Mystery, book 9
Mummy Pie Murder
A Freshly Baked Cozy Mystery, book 10
Wedding Bell Blunders
A Freshly Baked Cozy Mystery, book 11
In a Jam
A Freshly Baked Cozy Mystery, book 12
Tarts and Terror
A Freshly Baked Cozy Mystery, book 13
Fall for Murder
A Freshly Baked Cozy Mystery, book 14
Web of Deceit
A Freshly Baked Cozy Mystery, book 15

A Gracie Williams Mystery Series
Pushing Up Daisies in Arizona,
A Gracie Williams Mystery, Book 1
Kicked the Bucket in Arizona,
A Gracie Williams Mystery, Book 2

A Home Economics Mystery Series
Appliqued to Death
A Home Economics Mystery, book 1

Made in the USA
Las Vegas, NV
19 January 2024

84597725R00080